Assured Attention

Assured Attention

Jane Tulloch

To Bobbesse

Jane Tulloch

Comely Bank Publishing

This edition published 2017
by Comely Bank Publishing

This is a work of fiction. Names, characters, businesses, places,
events and incidents are either the products of the author's
imagination or used in a fictitious manner.

Cover design by Kit Foster Designs
Text printed in Adobe Garamond Pro and Calibri

ISBN: 978-0-9930262-3-2

This book is dedicated to my family, friends and felines,
some of whom are all three.

Contents

Chapter 1

Rosehill 'Revels'

Margaret Murray, woke with a start. She had slept fitfully all night, tossing and turning irritably. The harder she tried to sleep the more it had eluded her. Something was on her mind. The tendency for relatively minor concerns to take on epic proportions in the dead of night was never more obvious to her. Nevertheless, she worried. Now awake, her eyes wandered towards the windows shrouded in Murrays' best curtain fabric and plenty of it. Narrowing her eyes, she tried to perceive if the greyness filtering through the material was indicative of good or bad weather outside. It was too difficult to tell.

Curbing her first impulse to leap out of bed and get on with the day, she lay back and contemplated the day's activity and its implications. As proprietor, managing director and the latest in a family line of custodians, she had no doubt that Murrays of Edinburgh was a 'department store of distinction'. Murrays' proud boast was that it offered its best attention to all its customers. Time had moved on since she had inherited it from her father after the death of her brother. Life and the world of retail had changed, yet the store still tried its hardest to assure of its best attention. Not only that, she was aware of the immense contribution that the staff made towards this. It was important to recognise their efforts and to thank them. Hence, she had initiated a tea party some years ago to be held annually at Rosehill, her house on the edge of town. Today was the day once again. Margaret swung her legs over the edge of the bed and made her way across the deep carpet towards the window. Behind her, a black cat yawned and stretched on the bed, vaguely resentful of its rude awakening.

Throwing back the curtains she was unsure whether to be pleased or not. Certainly, it wasn't raining but neither did the grey sky look very promising either. She sighed. This was a big day at Rosehill. This much-anticipated event was known, ironically, to the staff as the Rosehill Revels. It was never exactly a wild affair consisting, as it usually did, of a thoroughly good tea and a walk around the gardens. It also provided the opportunity for staff to deck themselves in their best summer outfits, butterflies emerging from their drab work clothes. Occasionally, a game of French cricket would be started by one or other of the managers, but Mr Glen, the gardener, took a very dim view indeed of any damage to his precious flower beds so any such game tended to be somewhat subdued.

Looking down, Miss Murray could see the work going on in readiness for the great occasion. The invasion of several hundred people to the gardens necessitated a good deal of preparation. Mrs Glen, her elderly housekeeper and the wife of her gardener, had been a whirlwind of activity in the preceding week. It really was too much for her, Margaret thought, as she always did at this time. However, she was well aware that, despite her grumbling, Mrs Glen revelled in it all. She loved being indispensable and apparently doing the impossible by magicking up tea and cakes for the hungry hordes swarming all over her beloved Rosehill. She was fiercely protective of the place and a blizzard of notes forbidding entrance to various areas or indicating the presence of toilet facilities and, especially, signing the way to the exit were piled on the kitchen table before being affixed in the appropriate locations by the younger of the Joshi girls.

Breakfast was in the kitchen today. It was a rare treat for Miss Murray who was usually served her meals in solitary splendour in the dining room due to Mrs Glen's keen adherence to the standards previously set by Miss Murray's mother many years before. Breakfast today, however, was a riotous affair largely managed by Mrs Joshi and her two daughters: residents and keen assistants to Mrs Glen. They lived, along with Mr Joshi, in the lodge house. Mr Joshi worked in the Persian rug department at Murrays but helped Mr Glen with the gardening.

After the rather over-fried breakfast, Miss Murray wandered out to see what was going on in the garden. The triple garage had been cleared and bunting was being strung around its massive doors. Tea was to be served there in case of inclement weather, and little tables and chairs were being set out on the driveway and adjacent lawn. A number of the shop's younger male staff members had been roped into 'volunteering' to help set things up. It was a day out of the store, reasoned most of them, and they were happy enough to comply.

Mrs Glen, acting as commandant, was managing expertly to say just the wrong thing at the wrong moment to the wrong person. Sensing that the atmosphere was at risk of overheating, Miss Murray steered her old nanny towards the kitchen, saying that she must need that universal restorer, a 'nice cup of tea'. Mrs Glen grudgingly complied saying that her feet would be in enough trouble as it was by standing all afternoon at the tea urn. Miss Murray made soothing noises.

At 10.30am, Mrs Pegram, Mr McElvey and Barry Hughes arrived in Mr Philipson's car. These members of the management team had come early to help out. It was unlikely that they would be able to do much but their offer was appreciated. Barry, Head of Security, and Mr Philipson of Customer Services, immediately sat down and enjoyed a lengthy coffee break making a start on consuming the little cakes and home-made shortbread intended for the afternoon. Mrs Glen glared at them unnoticed then turned on her heel with a snort and went back to ordering people about in the garage.

Mrs Pegram from Personnel was a personal friend of Miss Murray and went in search of her. She wanted to check what her friend was planning to wear. Mr McElvey, the Finance Director, walked aimlessly around the garden deploring the waste of good commercial time that this afternoon's event represented. In the car on the way over, Mrs Pegram had tried to explain the value of staff 'feel-good' factor to him but to no avail. He fastidiously avoided talking to anyone as he walked towards the rose garden but became uncomfortably aware of being followed. On turning, he found Bluebell, Miss Murray's cat, studying him seriously. Looking about him to check that no one was watching, he leaned down to stroke the fluffy creature saying in an undertone, "Hello puss. Bit of an upset for you all this," and indicated the activity going on behind them. The black cat solemnly but silently agreed with him. The two moved on.

In a break from the usual pattern, Miss Murray had engaged a small band, "Teddy's Tunesters," to provide some music for the afternoon's event. The musicians' van drew up at the closed gate tooting its arrival. Mr Glen opened it for them. The van drove in and the band was informed that they would have to unload their equipment and take the van back outside onto the road as the driveway was being kept clear. Huffily, the band complied. Barry took over directing them confidently to the wrong location then, pretending that he'd known it all along, to the correct place with access to electric sockets for their amplifier. Mr McElvey frowned when he heard that this would be the sort of band which required amplification. Bluebell stalked away, tail twitching angrily, as the band began to tune up.

Meanwhile, tray after tray of tiny sandwiches, scones and miniature cakes was being carried out to the trestle tables in the garage. The urn had already been set up and the tea was now stewing away. Teacups and saucers had been set out in neat piles and jugs of orange juice stood ready for the non-tea drinkers. Miss Murray, Mrs Glen, Mrs Joshi and the girls had disappeared off to their rooms to change into their special party outfits. The men stood about awkwardly, mentally rehearsing the sorts of small talk they would be required to make with their staff members once the party started.

At 2.00pm on the dot the big gates to Rosehill swung open to reveal a short queue of ladies who had arrived a little too early and been uncertain as to how to proceed. They walked gratefully in towards the house noting the band playing under the trees and the little tables set out conveniently near the open garage doors sheltering the food and drinks. Some hesitated at this wondering if they should bag a table early or if that might look rude. Others, the newer members of staff, looked around them with undisguised inquisitiveness. So, this was the boss's house. Very nice too. They set off down the garden with the aim of trying to peer in the windows when no one was looking. There was something intrinsically fascinating about other people's houses.

One bright spark was unfortunate enough to remark to her friend from Ladies Gloves and Accessories, in the hearing of Mrs Glen, "I'm going to ask for the Ladies Room. I should be able to have a good look around once I'm inside the house."

The housekeeper, with pursed lips, silently

pointed to a notice indicating the way to a row of temporary conveniences discreetly located behind the garage. The crushed girl walked away with her head down. Her friends giggled.

In twos and threes, people began to drift in from the road. Soon, almost the entire staff complement had arrived and was milling about the garden. The sheer volume of chatting increased and at times almost drowned out the band. The band rose to the occasion as Teddy was keen to give value for money. He turned up the amplification which meant that the people were forced to talk even more loudly as they exchanged desultory small talk.

"SO HOW LONG HAVE YOU BEEN WORKING IN LADIES SEPARATES NOW?" Miss Murray found herself bellowing manfully as she tried to keep up an encouraging conversation with one of the younger staff.

"Six months," the overwhelmed girl whispered in reply, "but I'm leaving next week."

"LOVELY. GLAD TO HEAR IT," came the boomed response to the startled girl.

"This is ridiculous," thought Miss Murray and looked about her for assistance.

Barry, ever ready to rise to the occasion, rushed to her aid.

"ANYTHING I CAN DO?" he bawled. With an irritated wave of her hand Miss Murray indicated the band.

"OH," he instantly understood, or thought he did, "YOU'VE GOT A REQUEST FOR THEM?

WHAT WOULD YOU LIKE? SOMETHING SUMMERY?"

"I JUST WANT THEM TO BE QUIETER," she shouted.

"WHAT?"

"I JUST WISH THEY'D SHUT UP!" she continued, unfortunately coinciding with the band coming to the end of a set. Everyone stared at Miss Murray apparently loudly telling Barry to "shut up" in the momentary silence. She and Barry exchanged confused looks then rapidly went their separate ways, Miss Murray towards the band to ask them to lower the volume, and Barry to seek solace and tea from Mrs Pegram who could be seen laughing in the background.

By 3.30 that afternoon almost everyone had consumed a substantial amount of tea, sandwiches and cakes and were beginning to wonder what to do next. Teddy had whipped the Tunesters into a lather as they continued to belt out light classics as they called the middle of the road music they were known for. They were keen for a break and the drummer had noted ruefully that the supply of comestibles was rapidly reducing. He had been promised a good tea at this gig. To everyone's relief, they came to the end of their latest set and announced in echoing tones that they were taking a break. Conversation now became much more relaxed, not to mention, audible.

Most staff groups had resolutely stuck together, Ladies Separates with Ladies Separates, Shoes with

Shoes etc. The Tea Room staff had hovered disapprovingly eyeing the tea service going on at the garages. "Are those scones smaller than the ones that we serve?" wondered one. Several tutted at the dripping tap on the urn, "You'd think they would have fixed that," sniffed another. "And just look at that cloth!" Overhearing this, Mrs Joshi, abashed, removed the offending article from view and then wiped the urn's tap as discreetly as she could.

Mr Da Costa from Model Gowns, as expected, stood slightly aloof, uncertain how to interact with others on this intensely social occasion. Knowing how hard he found such situations, his colleague Mrs Hope gently steered him towards the tea tables. There she encouraged him to ferry trays of tea to older ladies gratefully taking the (often considerable) weight off their hardworking feet. With a clear task to do he was much happier and appreciated that there was no requirement for small talk.

Staff from the areas of the store involved in packaging and dispatch and who usually worked in the subterranean depths of the store wandered around blinking in the unaccustomed natural daylight. The gardeners among them taking an interest in Mr Glen's pride and joy: his herbaceous border. He policed this assiduously. At last year's tea party, he had caught Mrs Garland taking surreptitious cuttings from his best plants.

'Menswear' staff wandered around looking very bored. They would all have preferred to be at the football or at least watching sport on television.

They couldn't even have a kick about with the porters here. However, their respective better halves had insisted: their husbands must attend.

"A free tea at her place? It's the least she can do!" one wife had snapped, stung at being excluded from the invitation. Due to sheer weight of numbers, only staff members were invited. Many of the wives and, especially, the mothers, would have loved a good look around Miss Murray's home.

Gradually, there developed a palpable feeling of the afternoon coming to an end. Barry agitatedly wondered how they usually got rid of them all. He went over to Mrs Pegram to ask. Mrs Pegram was deep in conversation with Mr Morrison from Display and Advertising. Barry narrowed his eyes, Mr Morrison was a single man in his forties – competition! He clenched his jaw as he saw her laugh heartily at something Mr Morrison said. He wasn't to know that Mr Morrison was resolutely not a marrying man.

At 4.30 Miss Murray caught Mr Glen's eye and nodded. Giving a responding nod, he walked slowly over to the big gates which had been closed to provide privacy for the tea party. He opened them smoothly and clipped them back into place. Imperceptibly, and with nothing being said, people began to look at their watches and think about bus timetables. There was a concerted move to the conveniences prior to departure to, for some, longish journeys across town. A series of small contingents of the older staff members and those with better manners made their way towards Miss Murray to thank her for her hospitality. She graciously accepted their thanks and pressed them to return next year. With assurances that they would, they too, took their leave.

By 5.00pm it was all over for another year. Already tired out, Mrs Glen proceeded to supervise the dismantling of the tea area. Unsurprisingly, most of the morning's helpers had departed feeling that they had 'done their bit'. The Management team itself was then pressed into service. Mr Philipson and Mr Soames exchanged grimaces as they toiled to and fro carrying piles of little chairs. Pleading a bad back, Mr McElvey, carried empty plates one, at a time, to the kitchen where Mrs Joshi and the girls were up to their elbows in suds as they washed up the mountains of teacups and saucers. Barry had decided to patrol the precinct to check that everyone had actually left and that no one was hiding in any of the out buildings with evil intent. He would have been most disconcerted to hear Mrs Pegram tell Miss Murray, "Of course Barry's skiving again."

Miss Murray nodded unconcerned as she watched Teddy's now irritable Tunesters pack up their instruments and equipment. Not a success, she thought. She wouldn't be booking them again next year.

Later on, in the library, sitting companionably with throbbing feet on a shared low stool, Miss Murray and Mrs Pegram considered the afternoon. They were enjoying well deserved glasses of Chablis. Mr McElvey, very much at home at Rosehill, was in charge of dispensing large glasses of whisky to the menfolk. They talked of this and that in a tired way but were all pleasantly aware that the afternoon had gone quite well. They had done their duty for another year. Nobody could say that it had been exciting but honour had been satisfied and the staff had been offered and apparently enjoyed Miss Murray's hospitality.

The Glens and the Joshis had been stood down for the day after their strenuous efforts. The question of dinner arose and Barry had been sent out for fish and chips all round. On his return with this large order they were all called to kitchen to consume it direct from the packaging (to Mrs Glen's acute discomfiture). As they sat around the big scrubbed table consuming this feast, Miss Murray stood up and raised her glass somewhat unsteadily as she'd had a few too many.

"I just want to say thank you all for all your efforts today, and every day at Murrays. And at Rosehill too of course. I don't know how I could do without you all." Mrs Glen sniffed, Mrs Joshi looked down modestly but the girls looked up and smiled warmly.

Miss Murray raised her glass once more, "Here's to next year!"

"To Murrays and all who sail in her!" cheered Barry. The others frowned, briefly confused at this somewhat mixed metaphor, then smiled and clinked their glasses.

"To Murrays!"

Chapter 2

The Ladies' Man

Harry Ferguson, known to all as Flash Harry, had worked in Murrays since he had left school. He didn't work there because he liked it or wanted to, but because his long-widowed grandmother had insisted on it. For her, as for most grandmothers in the area, Murrays was quite the only place to aim for from a career point of view – and most other points of view too. Mrs Ferguson senior, as she preferred to be called as opposed to old Mrs Ferguson, had brought up Harry since he came into the world kicking, screaming and unwanted by his mother: a very fleeting girlfriend of her seagoing son. Mrs Ferguson had been taken aback one night to open her door to a red-faced, shouting man who thrust the infant Harry into her arms saying "Take him. He's your laddie's and we're no' having him."

The gallant Mrs Ferguson had risen to the occasion and, with the help of her other elderly friends, Mrs McNichol, Mrs Jarvis and Mrs Stevenson, had done her very best to give the boy a good start in life. These ladies had walked the floor with him as a baby, picked him up when he fell over when learning to walk and encouraged his earliest attempts at talking. As a boy, Harry had lacked for nothing, in the way of nourishing stews and good home baking. Similarly, hand-knitted jumpers and scarves were produced in profusion by them all and the little group of ladies cheered him on enthusiastically from the touchline at school football matches and proudly applauded his every brief appearance in school concerts. His end of term reports were eagerly awaited and perused by them all. Mrs McNichol helped him with arithmetic, Mrs Jarvis with English grammar and Mrs Stevenson took him to the library every week. His grandmother ensured that his homework was always done to her complete satisfaction. The late arrival of this child to raise brightened up all their lives.

Of course, this was a generation of ladies who would no more praise a child than fly in the air. Modesty, honesty and hard work were the precepts underpinning their approach to life. Harry grew up quite sure that, *"no one's looking at you"*, *"children should be seen and not heard"*, and that bodily functions should never, ever be discussed under any circumstances. Nevertheless, despite the apparently strict attitude of this committee of ladies who brought him up, he was always aware that he was deeply loved and cared for by them all. They each spoiled him with little secret treats; sugary tablet from Mrs Stevenson, permission to stay up late to watch TV on Mrs McNichol's watch, games of Ludo and Snap with Mrs Jarvis when he should have been doing his homework and huge, silent hugs from his grandmother when no one else was looking.

He wasn't really aware of how different his upbringing was until he reached senior school where his unconventional family of old ladies was remarked upon in less than complimentary terms by other, bigger boys. At first, he fought them back but it soon came to his attention that there was a group of giggling girls who always sprang to his defence. One, Big Norma, weighed in to save him from a particularly unpleasant encounter with Big Craig and sent Harry's would-be assailant off with his tail between his legs. The girls shouted most unladylike comments after the retreating lad and his cohorts. Now it seemed that Harry had acquired another group of females to look after him.

He grew into a rather handsome teenager and outside his home was always seen in the company of his clique of girls. They were not strictly speaking girlfriends in the accepted sense of the word (although Norma did harbour hopes in this direction), but his close circle of friends. Other boys were wary of them, frightened off by their sharply sarcastic tongues and focused jeering. Harry lorded over 'his' girls sure of their support and agreement in all matters. He learned a lot from them and was soon well versed in the manifold troubles facing young women today as well as all the latest views on hairstyles, make up, dance steps and who's who in pop music. With their help, his personal grooming was beyond reproach.

Despite the best efforts of the old ladies to encourage Harry to work hard at school, it soon became clear that he was not university material. In a way, this was a relief for the ladies who had been assiduously saving to fund his attendance at a university should the opportunity arise. They met one afternoon to discuss his future.

"Well, he'll no' be for the University anyway," said Mrs Jarvis sadly reading his latest school report. ("Struggling towards satisfactory", "Must try harder", "Poor concentration".)

"There's still time though," offered his Grandmother.

"Doesn't seem likely, not now he's found the lassies," Mrs McNichol added mournfully, "or rather now they've found him." This was something they all agreed on and regretted.

"He's an awful good looking laddie so you can't be too surprised at it." Mrs Stevenson didn't say much as a rule but when she did, they usually all agreed. They nodded sagely: old Mrs Ferguson particularly proudly.

"He could leave school this summer. What should he do?" Mrs Jarvis asked. The others stayed silent, pondering the problem.

"In my opinion, for what it's worth…" Mrs Jarvis began tentatively. They all looked doubtful but she continued nevertheless. "There would be no better place for a young man to start than at Murrays."

"They'd train him up and he could even get to be a manager one day," Mrs Ferguson put in. They all sighed wistfully at this lofty ambition. "They'd be lucky to have a good-looking boy like that. He'd be a credit to the store."

The nodding continued but they were all aware of the risk for big headedness and remained keen to make sure he knew his place. It was very important that he didn't get "beyond himself" as Mrs Ferguson had always put it.

Of course, thanks to his ring of girls, he was already far "beyond himself". Harry was now very sure of his extreme attractiveness to the opposite sex and had become something of a peacock. His interest in dress and fashion had grown immeasurably over the years and he became quite unable to pass a mirror without checking his reflection and making some minor alteration to his appearance. On one occasion when he was off school, a classroom wag (male) had remarked loudly that he must be off with a broken comb. Harry's girls had glared fiercely and the wag had quailed, rightly dreading break time.

The old ladies shook their heads. Despite their best efforts, Harry had become a completely, self-assured dandy. "Those girls!" they thought angrily, unaware that the atmosphere of care that they had created and their concerted attention to him when growing up, had itself contributed to the young man's immense self-possession.

Thus, it was an extremely smart and confident young man who faced Mrs Pegram at his interview for Murrays.

Mrs Pegram was immediately impressed by his immaculate appearance and how he was instantly at ease with her, unlike most of the young men she interviewed over the course of a year. She mentally pencilled him in for the management training scheme. She was happy to say that she would be delighted to offer him a position at Murrays. There were vacancies in the Food Hall, Ladies Separates and in Menswear. Given his extremely good presentation, it seemed entirely appropriate to assign him to Menswear. Harry was interested in this as he saw a good opportunity to equip himself with more smart clothes thanks to the staff discount. He presumed there would be one. However, on reflection, he decided that asking about it in his first interview might not look good so he didn't mention this intriguing possibility. Mrs Pegram arranged for him to start the following Monday.

The old ladies were thrilled for him and jubilant that the man they called "their boy" had secured what they saw as a prestigious position with good prospects. His younger circle of friends were less impressed.

"That old-fashioned place!" Norma burst out in disgust. "You'll be stuck with a bunch of old fogeys selling mackintoshes and leather gloves. God! You could have at least have got a job at C&A's then we could all get new things." The others joined in sneering at the uncool job their friend had taken.

Harry was momentarily nonplussed, caught again between the old ladies and the younger ones. He hung his head briefly before recovering his usual jaunty confidence. "I'll give them a go and see where it takes me," he said defiantly. "If it's just too boring I'll walk out." Although keen to impress the girls he still felt a deep affection and respect for the ladies who had brought him up so devotedly. He knew he owed them this opportunity to be proud of him.

The first few days in Menswear passed in a blur of impressions. So much new information to take in and systems to learn quite apart from navigating the geographical layout of the old shop. His feet and legs ached after a day of walking about the department, following other staff members to the store rooms to collect and unpack new stock, and even his break involved a long tramp up many flights of stairs to the staff canteen. He felt quite unable to answer the flurry of questions that greeted him on his return home.

The four old ladies were assembled expectantly, keen to hear all about every aspect of his day. All he wanted to know was whether there was sufficient hot water for him to have a long soak in the bath right now. After that he just wanted a plateful of his grandmother's restoring stew and to flop in front of the television, too tired even to phone Norma and the girls for the usual daily catch up. The ladies were nonplussed and looked at each other over their cups of tea.

"Surely it's not that hard work?" queried Mrs Stevenson.

"It can't be," replied Mrs McNichol.

Answering the phone to Norma, his grandmother took great satisfaction in telling her that Harry couldn't come to the phone as he was too tired to speak to her. Putting the phone down on

Norma's spluttering outrage Mrs Ferguson turned to the others,

"Well that's her gas at a peep anyway!" They nodded self-righteously. They still resented the hold the young group of girls held over him.

After his initial tiredness and the overwhelming nature of the new range of experiences he was facing died down a little, Harry was more able to think about the various aspects of his new life: for new life it was. Gone were the days of intense discussion with the girls about such topics as the uselessness of 'Rock Bottom' in the Eurovision song contest and the desirability of straight-legged jeans over flares. Additionally, there was no time for lengthy sessions involving tea and scones with the old ladies as they went over his apparently glowing prospects. Admittedly, he was glad not to have to hear them exchange the various inconvenient symptoms that seemed to go along with ageing in women. For the first time, however, he was resolutely in a world of men.

It wasn't that Menswear was an unattractive department. Located in the Grand Hall, it stretched out to a side door flanked by large windows. There were various sections within the department. Among these was one for Harris Tweed sports jackets and other casual outerwear including raincoats. There was a large display around a central glass case of shirts of all sorts: formal, with and without detachable collars, short and long sleeved. The exclusive made to measure section took up space under the gallery and contained many books of wool, wool and cashmere and cashmere only fabrics for the discerning customer to choose from. The counter was typically festooned with measuring tapes, pins and all the impedimenta of a tailor's shop. Facing this counter across the Grand Hall and similarly tucked under the gallery was the gentlemen's underwear section. Here a wide variety of underwear in all shapes and sizes was discreetly displayed on improbably endowed plaster models and otherwise safely stowed in a bank of glass-fronted drawers. There were rails and rails of trousers and slacks in a worrying variety of sizes. Harry found himself wondering who could possibly require trousers of such enormous waist sizes and short leg lengths. Ties, gloves, scarves, golf umbrellas, cuff links and other more minor but vital gentlemen's requirements were distributed in various logical nooks and crannies throughout the department.

It was a world populated almost exclusively by men selling items designed only for men. To Harry, it seemed the clothes in Menswear were designed mostly for *old* men but even the more modern stock left him cold. In fact, the other staff left him cold too. Out in the cold. He seemed to have nothing in common with any of them. Initial conversational forays related to enquiries as to what team he supported. Once it was established that he had no interest in football, motor racing, horse racing or even golf, he was regarded with some suspicion. In a muttered aside to old Mr Smith the specialist in measuring and fitting in the tailoring section, Mr Clark, the recently promoted senior sales assistant, was overheard, casting aspersions on Harry's sexual orientation. His smart appearance and comparatively high standards of personal grooming seemed to them to confirm this suspicion. Thereafter, he was aware of the others either avoiding him or stopping talking as he approached.

For the first time in his whole life, Harry felt uncomfortable. He was used to being popular and for his company to be sought out. He felt aggrieved that his undoubted skills were not appreciated here. He could identify, at a glance, the correct colour or style for a person but this was all too obviously of no interest to the male customers who would back away if he made suggestions such as, "Sir, avoid wearing eau de nil as it is so draining." Nor was the fact that he could strike up conversation on a wide variety of topics (except sport of any kind of course) appreciated. He was knowledgeable and up to date on current affairs: he knew which celebrity or minor member of the Royal family was engaged and to whom. Pop music held no mysteries for him, and his hitherto widely acclaimed dancing skills were of no interest to staff or customers.

That the other members of staff enjoyed working there was apparent. Like most Murrays staff they made their own entertainment. Small wagers were made as to the likelihood of Mr Clark being able to persuade a certain reluctant customer to buy a hideous jacket that they'd been trying to get rid of for years. Scraps of paper with unlikely names and telephone numbers would be slipped into newly purchased trouser pockets, "for a laugh," Harry was told. He didn't find that very funny as he contemplated the notes being found by suspicious wives. Particularly jarring colour combinations were highlighted as the very latest and sold as such to less confident members of the public anxious to look up to date. How the staff laughed as the unfortunate customers concerned scuttled out of the side door. Harry found it impossible to join in the salacious comments about female customers or staff members. Somehow, it didn't feel right to him. Menswear seemed a harsh, unkind sort of place.

Although he was unpopular with the staff in Menswear, his good looks had made him the focus of a great deal of female attention. Girls from China and Glass or Linens would lean over the gallery banisters and feast their eyes on him. The bolder of them would send little notes fluttering down offering to meet him in the stock room. Looking up at one of the senders of these missives he blew a kiss to her. And so began his career as the Murrays' Casanova. As ever, the ladies loved him. This did not endear him to the male staff who, when it emerged that he was most certainly not gay, shunned him even more.

"Jealous I expect," opined Harry nonchalantly to his latest conquest, Miss Reid from the Shoe department. She agreed, basking in her position as his girlfriend du jour. Norma was not happy. His female coterie was growing out of her control. She even confided this to Mrs Ferguson during a phone call she had made trying to catch Harry in.

"Never mind dear," Mrs Ferguson had said kindly, "A boy like him was always going to be popular."

Despite his growing number of female fans, Harry spent long, lonely, tedious days at work. He began to alarm his Grandmother with his deep sighs and clear reluctance to go to work. Some days it took two of the old ladies to force him to eat some breakfast and run for the bus. He was noticeably dejected. He would pace about the large department regarding the racks of jackets, cabinets of jumpers and rows of ties with loathing. He grew to hate and despise the entire stock. The underwear in the discreet drawers, the displays of dull shirts and so-called leisure gear seemed to underline everything that he disliked in the department. He couldn't imagine anyone wanting to wear any of it. He tried to engage with ladies who came to choose items as presents for husbands or sons. They would often ask his advice.

"What would you choose? You're about the same age as my nephew," asked one perfectly pleasant woman.

It was unfortunate that his response of, "Well not *that* anyway," was overheard by Mr Clark. He was severely reprimanded and told to remember that he was in Murrays and owed each customer his best attention,

"Your best attention son, or you're oot," he finished with a curt nod.

Harry nodded back miserably.

And he was miserable. As the weeks went on and grew into months he became more and more disconsolate. He would rally occasionally, buoyed up by a pep talk from the old ladies or by the sight of the girls parading past the windows making faces and gesticulating at him. He would decide to smarten up his attitude and try to chat to his co-workers. He did face a major setback, however, when he was unfortunate enough to witness the unexpected and fatal arrival of a young store detective pushed to his death from an upstairs gallery. The poor young man's fall had ended in a glass display cabinet. Unsurprisingly, Harry and all the floor staff were very shocked and distressed. This ghastly event did serve as an unlikely catalyst though.

Mrs Pegram from Personnel, keen as ever to support her staff, had been drawn to the Grand Hall in the aftermath of the accident. She wanted to check that everyone had recovered at least a little from the shock of it all. Everyone was sent home on the day but were expected back at work the next day. Mr Clark reassured her that they were all fine with one exception: Harry. He indicated the young man idly rearranging socks. "He's not much use today," he said, "or any day either."

Noticing Harry's pallor, she walked over to him. "Good morning Mr Ferguson or can I call you

Harry?" she queried.

"Oh, hello Mrs Pegram," he replied listlessly, putting the socks down.

"I was just wondering how you were after, you know, yesterday."

"Oh fine," he said with some asperity. "Well, no, now you mention it, I'm not fine. Not fine at all." He heaved an unexpected sigh that sounded suspiciously like a sob. Taking another look at him Mrs Pegram suggested that he come up to her office. Nodding at the other staff members who stood together watching what was going on, she took Harry by the arm and marched him up to the entrance of the staff staircase. He complied passively. "I suppose I'm fired," he thought glumly to himself. Then, in slight agitation, "Oh no! What will Gran say?"

In the office, he slumped down in a chair. To his surprise, Mrs Pegram didn't sit behind her desk but took a seat next to him. She recognised that there was more to this distress than might be expected. "What is it Harry?" she asked gently.

There was a long pause. She was about to reframe her question when he blurted out, "It's here. Just here. Being here in Murrays. I hate it, I hate it, I hate it."

He shook his head vehemently.

Taken aback Mrs Pegram replied, "I know yesterday was an awful shock for us all. That poor young man, but I expect you'll soon feel a bit better and enjoy getting back to work." He looked unconvinced.

"There's something about getting back into the old routine," she finished kindly.

He jerked his head back at that and turned to look very directly at her, "But that's just it! I don't like the 'old routine'. I don't want to do it anymore." With that he stood up and marched out. Mrs Pegram called after him but he didn't return nor did he go back to Menswear as she discovered when she phoned to check on how he seemed. Mr Clark was positively glowing when he happily informed her that no, young Mr Ferguson had not, apparently, found it necessary to return to his post. He then enquired whether or not he had been sacked.

"No. No, he hasn't. Let me have a think about it and I'll let you know." She sat back to have the promised think. After a while, she consulted a file then lifted the telephone.

Mrs Ferguson sat outside Mrs Pegram's office in some trepidation. Of course, she had sat outside a head teacher's office often enough waiting to be told that the school were disappointed in Harry in some way or another: insufficient effort in Maths, complaining about the school dinners or, worst of all, some form of impertinence. Always "disappointed" though. A particularly depressing word, she thought. She wondered what he'd done now. The door opened and a pleasant smiling woman emerged.

"Mrs Ferguson, thank you so much for coming. I'm Mrs Pegram," the smiling woman introduced herself. "Do come in."

Mrs Ferguson entered the small cluttered office cautiously, still waiting for trouble. However, she was surprised when Mrs Pegram explained why she had requested the meeting.

"We were very pleased with your Harry when he first joined us. Such a smart young man. But something seems to have happened to him. I know he was, naturally, very upset at the tragic incident which he most unfortunately witnessed but it seems to go beyond that. He tells me that he's very unhappy in Murrays. I wondered if you could cast any light on that?" She finished hopefully.

"Oh," responded Mrs Ferguson in surprise. Her first instinct was to deny that Harry had any problems at all but, on seeing Mrs Pegram's concerned expression, she relented. With a sigh, her face relaxed and she replied, "No, you're right. There's something wrong with the laddie. He's not himself."

"Any idea what it might be? I don't want to pry into personal matters but is there, maybe, anything going on at home that might be upsetting him?

"No, not that I can think of. Mrs McNichol is going for a hip replacement and he was concerned about that and Mrs Stevenson's not what she was."

She paused while they both thought about that. Then she continued: "He's not got the time he had for Norma and the gang from school of course."

"Now, who are all these people?" enquired Mrs Pegram, "Relatives? Friends?"

"Well, Mrs McNichol and Mrs Stevenson are friends of mine who more or less helped me to bring Harry up. He was just left with me you know," she confided. "I had to just get on with it. Mrs Jarvis helped too of course. We all did our best and he's not turned out badly?" she finished plaintively. "We're all very proud of him."

"Oh, undoubtedly," Mrs Pegram responded, nodding her head vehemently. "I take it Norma's a girlfriend?"

"No. Well, not exactly. To let you understand," she continued, using the time-honoured Scottish phrase. "She's a girl, they all are, his school friends I mean, but they're not 'girlfriend' girlfriends if you know what I mean." She stuttered to a halt, eyebrows raised, willing Mrs Pegram to understand what she meant.

"I see," said Mrs Pegram, sitting back in her chair reflectively. "Tell me, do you think there's something about the department he works in that he doesn't like? Is it the people there or the stock maybe?"

"Maybe," Mrs Ferguson ventured cautiously, having wondered about that too.

"Look, I'll have a think about this, tell him to come and see me first thing on Monday."

The two ladies looked at each other and nodded, their thoughts taken up by the problem of what to do with Harry.

The following Monday a somewhat subdued Harry presented himself at Mrs Pegram's door.

"Come in Harry," her disembodied voice called out.

He entered and found Mrs Pegram standing at an open filing cabinet, a file in her hand.

"Sit down Harry." He took a seat.

"Now," she said turning to look at him. "I gather that you're not altogether happy in your current department."

"Well. I don't know." Harry had never really thought about this as a possibility. He didn't really like it and felt excluded by the other men but had just accepted the situation passively. He'd just put up with it.

"Would you like a move?" she suggested.

"Oh. Gosh. Where to?" His mind reeled as he contemplated the sort of department that were usually staffed by men. He wasn't thrilled at the prospect of Ironmongery or Electrical. He'd struggle to be interested in Furniture or even the Food Hall.

"I was wondering about Ladies Separates actually," Mrs Pegram continued smoothly. "I gather that you have an eye for matching clothes, colours and so on. How would you feel about that? We don't usually place male staff there but something tells me that you might fit in well there. The ladies are a friendly bunch – and I hear you are a bit of a ladies' man," she added teasingly.

He reddened but was undeniably interested in the prospect. He already had some friends in that department and the Ladies Outdoor clothing department which abutted it.

"Oh, that would be," he corrected himself, "could be terrific. In fact, I think I'd like that. Yes, please." He inwardly rebuked himself for such an uncool response but couldn't help himself. It was a wonderful prospect. To be back among the sort of people he was most comfortable with, to be able to share in their conversations and to be complimented on his work (which would be beyond reproach he told himself) would be such a relief.

The news of his transfer went down well in several quarters: Menswear were delighted to see the back of him, but he was welcomed by all in Ladies Separates (and Ladies Outdoor clothing, Swimwear and even Model Gowns if truth be told).

Safely installed, Harry himself was once more surrounded by a circle of friendly females. He was very happy.

To the irritation of his "girlfriend du jour", Norma and the gang were frequent poppers in and were encouraged to try on various unlikely items for fun. His grandmother and the elderly ladies were often accommodated in the backroom and surreptitiously plied with tea and biscuits carefully carried down from the canteen to revive them from strenuous shopping expeditions.

Nor was this transfer a one-way street for Murrays. Harry proved to be a very able member of staff and his suggestions and personal attention went down very well with customers. His eye for colour and style was noted by the Management and he was once more pencilled in for a place on the Management training course.

The Ladies' man was back where he had always been: with the ladies.

Chapter 3

A Renaissance

Hard as it was to imagine Mr McElvey, Murrays' Finance Director, having sprung from an actual family, it was a biological fact that he had. His parents, now late, had lived a quiet life of unimpeachable respectability in relative financial security. His father approved of his son's transition from the grammar school into a world of figures; what his mother thought was of no relevance in their stern Calvinist household. Life for the McElveys had been a daily striving and suppression of selfish impulses. Regrettably, this had gone along with a strong tendency to deplore those less well off than themselves and to blame the less fortunate for their own misfortunes.

Charity, such as it was, strictly began at home for the McElveys.

In this stronghold of self-denial and general misery, there was one jarring note – Mr McElvey's sister Norah. She was ten years younger than him and her arrival had been a huge surprise for all concerned. From the start, she was so different from the rest of her family that she was considered by her West Highland Free Presbyterian mother to be a changeling. Her less fanciful father was quite sure they had been given the wrong baby on discharge from the maternity hospital. However, her strong physical resemblance to her progenitors disproved this. Where their sharp features appeared stern on both parents and elder brother, on Norah's little face they looked positively pixyish.

Little Norah would have been a joy in any other family. She had an infectious smile which turned rapidly into a bubbling laugh. She loved nothing more than to dance and sing and was generally a tremendous source of embarrassment for her family. Nor did she change as she grew up. She was popular at school with both pupils and staff and her irrepressible good humour appeared incapable of being curbed by the intense disapproval she daily experienced at home.

At the same time that her newly qualified older brother was settling into his job at Murrays, Norah's talent as an artist began to emerge. Her head teacher pleaded with her parents to allow her to attend the Art College, but they were adamantly against such frivolity.

"Norah is to be a teacher or a nurse," her father stated with some finality. As a placatory gesture, he continued, "Of course she may draw her wee pictures in her spare time."

The head teacher sighed. Poor Norah, she thought. This was the general consensus in the staff room. All the teachers wanted to help Norah, but it was not to be. She was duly enrolled at the local teacher training college despite her lack of aptitude in this field.

The summer before she started college, Mr McElvey found her a temporary job at Murrays. He was pleased that she seemed to accept this so well at a time when her friends were either off on exotic foreign holidays or lounging at home playing tennis and swimming every day. Norah put her head down and worked hard in the packing department. She didn't chat or distract others and was always open to working overtime. Mr McElvey was gratified that she was such a credit to him. Her parents felt she had settled down at last and they relaxed their iron discipline sufficiently to allow her some time to herself and to keep her meagre earnings.

"It'll be good for her to see what it takes to earn a living," her father told her mother. "We'll not be here forever and she'll need to find her own way in life." His wife nodded.

Thus, it was a huge surprise to them all when she did indeed find her own way in life. She found her own way all the way to Australia. The first they knew of this was one Sunday when she didn't appear for breakfast before church. On finding her empty room and a short note saying she was leaving, they were devastated. A thousand questions flooded in. Where could she have gone? Who knows about this? What should we do? A long night followed as the three considered the situation. The McElveys were as one in their desire to keep the police out of it. "What would the neighbours think?" was a key imperative. They waited for her to return home chastened by her experience, but this was not to be. Norah had escaped.

In time, they discovered that she was in

Melbourne. Letters arrived at six-monthly intervals but, naturally, her parents didn't respond. It was only when they had both expired (of influenza in their unheated, cheerless house) and Mr McElvey junior was going through their papers that he found the small packet of airmail letters. From these he gathered that Norah was now married to a prosperous builder called Bruce and was mother to three sons and a daughter. His eyes glistened as he examined a photograph enclosed in the most recent communication. The family smiled out at him, a vision of suntanned vigour and cheerful happiness. The strapping boys looked like rugby players and the girl like a cheerleader: all had healthy bronzed skin and plenty of excellent teeth displayed in wide smiles.

A happy looking family, he concluded gloomily and resolved to write to the latest address to inform Norah of her parents' death. She was not mentioned in Mr and Mrs McElvey's will, but he was quite prepared to do the decent thing and forward her share.

Norah responded quickly to the letter. To his amazement, she telephoned: an extravagance that shocked her brother.

He was startled to hear the breezy Australian voice say, "Jeez I guess I'm not surprised the oldies never changed their phone number! Hi, it's me Norah!"

They talked briefly of business matters. She shrugged off his offer of half the inheritance, saying,

"It's quite OK. It's good of you, but Bruce has done well and we really don't need any more."

He felt tempted to question this, but held himself back.

She continued, "We may be able to set up the kids too. Why don't you just keep it for your own family?"

He told her stiffly that he had no family, having never married (a pre-requisite for Scottish McElveys). He winced as she expressed surprise.

"Gee why the hell not, you old dog? Got a chick on the side? One Ma and Pa never got to hear about?" she teased.

Tautly, he denied this and outlined his proposed new living arrangements: he would sell the family house and invest the money, using the income to offset the expense of living in a residential club near Murrays. There he would be fully looked after and would not have to worry about maintaining a house, shopping, cleaning, laundry and all the sundry activities of running a home. He was looking forward to it. All Norah said was a heartfelt, "Strewth!"

Further pleasantries were exchanged and the call came to an end. As he hung up he felt a tiny pang of something that he would much later recognise as loneliness.

The move to the club was a great success. It was conveniently located for his work at Murrays, negating the need for a car. The food was excellent, the housekeeping department understood his laundry and cleaning requirements and he felt quite at home in the starchy atmosphere of the club drawing room and bar. This club was very much for 'those and such as those' and, should he feel the need for company, there was always a polite acquaintance to talk to. He settled in very well.

The years passed and he never met anyone he wanted to settle down with or felt the need to set up home elsewhere; he remained a fixture at the club. At breakfast one grey morning, as he was gloomily contemplating his usual single poached egg, he became aware of a disturbance at the entrance to the dining room. As he had assiduously avoided looking up, he was surprised to hear a discreet cough at his side from Simpson the Head Porter.

"Do excuse me sir, but a young person is asking to see you. I have informed her that you are currently occupied, but she is most insistent I inform you of her presence."

"A young person? Are you quite sure it is me she is looking for? I can't think who it could be. It must be some mistake," he said dismissively, turning back to his plate.

"No mistake Uncle Ian," said a loud voice across the expanse of carpet. Other silent breakfasters looked up askance. With a sigh, he threw down his napkin and strode across the room. To his horror, as he arrived in her proximity, she started forward and threw her arms around him, shouting, "Uncle Ian, I can't believe it's you! You look just like Mum said you would."

With an inward groan he realised this must be his Australian niece. He had almost forgotten his conversation with his sister so many years ago. Indicating irritably that she should follow him, he abandoned his breakfast with some regret.

They went to the empty drawing room. It was cold in there and they sat near the window at the young woman's request, "Want to catch some rays after all, Unc."

He winced. "May I offer you some refreshment?" he asked politely but distantly. "Some tea perhaps?"

"Any chance I could get a big pot of coffee and a snag?"

"A what?" he asked faintly.

"Sorry Unc, I mean a sarnie? A bacon roll? Whatever you guys eat at breakfast?" she continued.

"I daresay they might find you some tea and toast." He quelled her with a look.

Crestfallen and suddenly very tired after her long flight, she slumped in her seat. "OK Unc, whatever."

He signalled to the hovering waitress and made his request.

Over an awkward breakfast, the story emerged. Despite her informing him that she was called Sam, he persisted, to her growing irritation and weariness, in calling her Samantha. Samantha had embarked, with her mother's encouragement, on a trip home to the old country, as she persisted in calling it. She had assumed she would be welcomed by her uncle and, naturally, she would stay with him.

With a sinking heart Sam began to realise that the old guy of her imaginings bore no resemblance to the person now examining her with some distaste. She gulped down the lukewarm tea, coughing a little over the dry toast crumbs, and said sadly, "Well I guess I'm not really welcome here." She stood up and began to gather her assortment of rucksacks and bags together.

With a sigh, Mr McElvey, realising that he had some responsibility for this young family member, reassured her. "No, no, you just took me by surprise that's all. I'll see if I can organise accommodation for you for a few nights." He stood up and walked across the room towards the door. Looking back at her he took in her crumpled rather grubby appearance and sighed again. He told himself that she had, after all, just travelled half way around the world so she was probably very tired and in need of a rest.

Arrangements were made for the short-term occupancy of a single room at the club and they arranged to meet at 6pm. This would give her time for a bath and a good sleep and him time to put in a day's work at Murrays. Sam hoped they would both feel a little more relaxed later.

Her uncle's thoughts were less charitable. By the time they met up again that evening, they'd both had time to think. Sam was much the better for a long sleep and a short bath. Mr McElvey was rather tired after an irritating day at work: things had not gone his way at the management meeting and he was mentally formulating a response.

Sam greeted him cheerfully. "Hi there Uncle Ian." She called out across the library bar. She remembered her mother's instructions: she was to brighten up the old guy and try to get him to change his old-fashioned ways. Looking at him now as he picked his way irritably between the tables, she doubted that such a task would be possible, but, nevertheless, she was game.

"So Unc. What's the plan for tonight?"

"The plan?" He replied. "Dinner of course. It will be served at 7.30."

He continued hospitably, "Now, may I offer you a glass of sherry?"

"I'd rather have a beer if they've got it Unc." She countered.

"Beer?"

"Yes, a bottle if poss."

"It certainly won't be poss, er possible. I'll just ask for my usual. I trust that will do?" He raised his eyebrows.

Humbled, she agreed. He nodded over to the watching barman and two small glasses of dry sherry were brought to their table.

Over the formal dinner in the dining room he interrogated her on her past, her immediate plans and her long-term prospects. He was startled to find that she had no particular plans other than to "hang around Scotland for a while." He persevered. Surely she had a university place waiting for her? Apparently not. She was just like her mother he eventually concluded. Australia was probably the best place for her.

Sam was a little hurt at his keenness for her to return and explained that she had an open ticket and could remain for a short while at least. Perhaps she could visit him at work? He was appalled by the prospect. In her current clean but decidedly shabby state, she would not be a credit to him. He simply didn't know what to do with this unexpected, unwanted visitor. The unfortunate young woman quite suddenly became more than a little hurt and, in her surprise, tiredness and culture shock, she began to cry. Scotland was nothing like the sunny, happy life she was accustomed to and had foolishly expected to find.

Mr McElvey had no experience in dealing with weeping women and he was embarrassed to be seen with one by the other club members. The staff were plainly enthralled at this drama involving the stuffiest member of the stuffy club. He suggested she have an early night and retired to his room to ponder the dilemma.

He was surprised to be joined by her at breakfast the next morning, but jet lag had struck and she was wide awake. Mr McElvey had thought long and hard during the night and had come to certain conclusions. These he outlined to her over his usual single poached egg. He noted that Samantha's appetite was not affected by her jet lag and she consumed enormous quantities of bacon and eggs. His plan was to take a week's annual leave and introduce her to her Scottish cultural heritage. He had meticulously drawn up a programme of visits to art galleries, museums and concerts. Fortuitously, Scottish Opera were performing this week and the club concierge had already been despatched to collect tickets for two performances. Mr McElvey was very pleased with his plan and felt that no uncle could be expected to do more. He was actually looking forward to it.

Sam was appalled. She could think of nothing more boring than the planned activities. Remembering her mother's strict instructions to, "lighten the old guy up," she could not see how she possibly could under these circumstances. However, she nodded politely "Sure thing Unc. Sounds good."

He winced. "Please, I must ask you to refrain from calling me that name." He couldn't bring himself to say it aloud.

"I would prefer it if you would call me Uncle Ian," he stated clearly.

"OK Uncle Ian," she said humbly. "When do we start the cultural bonanza?"

"I will need to make arrangements at work so I'll have to go in today, but I expect that we could start tomorrow." He examined his programme, "Yes, it's the National Gallery in the morning and the Portrait Gallery in the afternoon. Then we have *The Marriage of Figaro* in the evening."

"Oh goody," she said "A wedding! Have we been invited?"

He sighed as he pointed out that it was an opera

not a social function. He had a thought. "Do you have more suitable clothes with you?"

"What do you mean?" she asked, "These are my best jeans and my warmest top."

"Well, you'll have to do better than that." He thought for a moment, "I'll ask Mrs Carr our secretary to take you around Murrays and choose some more appropriate outfits. Don't worry, I'll have them put on my account."

He stood up. "I'm off now, but if you come to my office in Murrays at, say, 11am I'll arrange for you and Mrs Carr to meet. She'll know what to do."

"See you there, Uncle Ian," came the reply. With a nod he set off across the dining room, pleased with his plans.

Mrs Carr was the secretary for Miss Murray and Mr McElvey. She had often been referred to as an excellent woman and, indeed, she was. A small, somewhat dumpy woman of indeterminate age, she always wore severe black suits for work, except on her birthday or other (not very) festive occasions, when she donned a navy blue one. She considered pearls to be 'de rigueur', something that she and Miss Murray very much agreed on. She was a very serious woman who applied the same serious attitude to her work. There was a Mr Carr and there was talk of her having a son, but neither were ever referred to nor had they ever been seen visiting the store. She was an enthusiastic teetotaller who had cast a dampener on many social occasions. Surprisingly, her main interest was the ups and downs of the London stock exchange, not that she had ever invested any money in shares or was ever likely to. She had explained this interest to Miss Murray as a form of, for her, inexpensive gambling. She enjoyed plotting what she would have gained or lost had she ever actually invested. If she was notably downcast on any day, Miss Murray would sympathetically ask, "Rio Tinto again? Or was it British Plasterboard?" Mrs Carr would shake her head miserably muttering, "I can't think why they went in for Sudanese alluvial minerals," or some such.

This, then, was the person Mr McElvey thought best placed to take his young niece around the shop to choose appropriate clothes.

At the appointed hour of 11am, she and Sam regarded each other with some misgiving. On her part, Mrs Carr was appalled. She could hardly believe Mr McElvey could be related to such a disreputable young person. Sam herself had made a real effort to smarten up and had gone so far as to tie her hair back with an elastic band. Mrs Carr had already made a short tour of appropriate departments and had identified some items that she thought suitable.

"Come along, let's go." She said briskly, "I can't spare much time."

The two set off down the stairs to Ladies Separates, Model Gowns and the Designer Rooms being thought too extravagant for such a young woman. Looking at Samantha some hours later, Mr

McElvey concluded that he had asked just the right person to guide his niece towards a more apposite style of dress. Not only had she two new suits with matching blouses, shoes and handbags, but a visit to Hairdressing had tamed her unruly locks to a considerable extent. Mrs Carr promised that they would go shopping again soon for, "weekend clothes," as she called them. This couldn't happen soon enough thought Sam unhappily. She was most uncomfortable in the stiff suit and blouse with its "charming" constricting pussycat bow at the neck. She longed for her jeans and tee shirt.

To the surprise of both Mr McElvey and Sam, their week of cultural pursuits went very well.

Sam found the art galleries most interesting and particularly liked the Scottish Colourists. She and her uncle (who naturally preferred eighteenth century Scottish artists) even enjoyed discussing artists over dinner in the evening. The opera visits did not go so well and even Uncle Ian had to admit they had not seen the operatic ensembles at their inspiring best. The Botanic Gardens were in full flower as they walked around and the view from the castle was much appreciated and exclaimed over. Scottish history intrigued Sam and Uncle Ian tracked down a series of open lectures at the University that she could attend while he was at work.

Sam did not forget her mother's instructions to try to, "lighten up Uncle Ian," and he did seem to be more cheerful as he threw himself into expanding her cultural horizons. This included discussions around differing social behaviour between Australian and Scottish cultures: what was and was not acceptable over here as opposed to over there was carefully outlined. After some initial protests, Sam took this on board. She stopped using certain words and phrases, reduced the volume of her speech altogether and became politer in general. This was not achieved without some strain.

They soon settled into a routine. Each morning, Mr McElvey went to work and Sam set off to the University or one of the museums; they would then meet to compare notes over dinner. Mr McElvey gradually began to talk more about his work and enjoyed the audience she provided as he outlined the various issues involved. He was surprised to find that she had a very good head for figures and was a fast learner. It became clear to his mind that she was a natural chartered accountant. This had never previously occurred to her, but, as he talked about it, she gradually saw that this could indeed be just the profession for her. Fancy me having a profession, she thought.

One evening, the two were invited to Rosehill for dinner. Miss Murray and Mrs Pegram were both intrigued to meet Mr McElvey's Antipodean niece. They had wondered what she might be like and Miss Murray, knowing of her housekeeper's standards, warned her that the young girl might be "not quite." Mrs Glen understood but did not necessarily approve.

They all expected an uncouth young person speaking in a marked Australian accent and using unfamiliar, potentially unsavoury, words. However, all of them were delightfully surprised by the tidy young woman who arrived with her uncle at the precise time they were invited. Sam was plainly on her best behaviour and trying her hardest to demonstrate her newly acquired social skills. She liked Miss Murray and Mrs Pegram and appreciated their efforts to draw her out and show an interest in her. The dinner party went very well and Miss Murray, impressed by the pleasantly demure young woman, found herself offering Miss Cooper a clerical job in the office; Mrs Carr needed an assistant. It was made clear to Miss Murray that this would be a temporary arrangement until such time as Miss Cooper started her accountancy course.

"Of course," Miss Murray responded, "and maybe when you've completed your training you can take over your uncle's job when he retires!"

They all laughed, except for Mr McElvey.

Several months later, Mr McElvey and Sam were having breakfast in the dining room of the club. They were both dressed in rather severe business suits and happily discussing the financial arrangements relating to the purchase of some new stock from Denmark. He was pleased to note that Samantha made some useful suggestions. Once more, there was a commotion at the door, but this time no staff member could check the rush of two casually dressed, middle-aged people as they careered towards the McElvey table.

"Sam, Sam," shouted the man.

"Over here doll!" called the woman, "Sam, Sammy it's us!"

"Oh God" said Sam. "It's Mum and Dad."

By this time the dishevelled couple had reached the table. Mr McElvey and Sam stood up awkwardly. The woman threw her arms around her daughter and the man enthusiastically pumped Mr McElvey's hand up and down. The other breakfasters stared at the scene unashamedly.

"Uncle Ian," said Sam politely, "these are my parents. May I introduce Bruce and Norah Cooper from Melbourne Australia?"

"Sam," said her mother, staring hard, "What's wrong with you?" She turned accusingly towards her brother "What have you done you bastard? Why is she speaking to me like that?" Mr McElvey winced at such strong language so freely introduced.

"Strewth, forget that," said Bruce, "What's she wearing for God's sake? That's not my Sammy," he said with some feeling.

"You know what?" said Norah, sagging down resignedly into a nearby chair.

"We sent her over here to change Ian. But instead he did it."

"Did what?" asked Mr McElvey.

"Turned her into a right McElvey, that's what!" she spat.

Sam wiped her mouth politely on her linen

napkin and, in an unconscious echo of the welcome she herself had received, said smoothly, "Now, Mum, I may I offer you some refreshment? Some tea perhaps?"

Chapter 4

Convenience

Elma looked at the letter in front of her with unseeing eyes, or at least eyes that refused to believe what they had just read. *£10,000 for me*, she thought. *Just me.* She shook her head as though to dissolve what she had read, but the words refused to disappear. It was plain that Mrs Elma Struthers had indeed won £10,000 on the Premium Bonds. She had completely forgotten the ten premium bonds her father had solemnly presented her with so many years ago. He would be so pleased, she mused. A small smile played over her careworn face. At last she let her heart leap as she pondered her good fortune. The money would allow her to give up work and tide her over until her pension was payable; it would even supplement the pension considerably if it was invested judiciously.

A whole new train of thought was set off: who would help her to invest it? Who could she, should she, trust? If only Tom was still alive. If only Matthew hadn't emigrated to Canada. Her heart leapt again. She could move to Canada! This new idea was just flooding her thoughts when there was a knock at the door.

"Excuse me," a disembodied voice asked "Is it possible to refill the soap dispenser? It seems to be empty."

Shaking herself from her reverie, Elma got heavily to her feet. She opened the hatch in the door to reveal a flustered face. "Of course," she replied. "With you in a minute," and, turning to the shelf behind her in her little cubby hole, she lifted down a tin of liquid soap. She bustled into the Ladies Room where a small group were clustered around the sinks.

"Do excuse me ladies," she called out, refilling the soap dispenser that had unaccountably emptied itself over the course of just one morning. She then topped up the other soap dispensers, and put the tin back in the cupboard. A quick check of the vacant cubicles to ensure all was well within and there was sufficient toilet paper set her mind at rest. She returned to her cubby hole to resume thinking.

Elma had started work early that morning, grabbing her letter from the postman as she rushed down her tenement stairs to catch the bus. Now, late morning, was the first opportunity she'd had to open her mail. The morning's work had been the usual flurry of cleaning, mopping and replenishing the various consumables provided in a ladies' 'cloakroom' as it was euphemistically called. As this was one of Murrays' ladies' cloakrooms, these consumables were rather more than just toilet paper and soap. Elma took enormous pride in her work and her 'cloakroom' was the convenience of choice for any lady coming into town. The immaculate sinks, each with sparkling taps, were interspersed with small vases of fresh flowers. Roller towels were replaced regularly and, for those who preferred not to use the communal rollers, discreet napkins were folded in neat piles in front of the gleaming mirrors.

The soap in the shining dispensers was delicately scented and resolutely not the usual utilitarian cleaning product found in bathrooms.

The ladies' cloakroom at Murrays didn't just offer an opportunity for the obvious convenience: chairs were placed at the mirrors to allow exhausted customers a short respite and this was a popular resting place for those unfortunate ladies who needed a break but couldn't quite rise to the prices in the tea room. Elma knew this coterie very well and kept a kettle in her cubby hole, judiciously supplying refreshingly strong cups of tea to those that she deemed in need.

Elma herself was an institution. She had worked in the Ladies Room for the past twenty-five years. In that time, she had been witness to many of life's ups and downs. She still remembered the day when Mrs Potter, a long-term customer, remained a bit too long in the end cubicle. Elma had waited for a lull in ladies' use of the facilities before whispering, "Mrs Potter? Are you all right?"

After receiving no response to her increasingly urgent enquiries, she had responded to the ultimate dilemma presented to any ladies' room attendant by whisking out her pass key and carefully opening the door. Mrs Potter was found to be at her final rest in this, the rest room at Murrays. It was as it should be, thought Elma, as she gently closed her oldest customer's eyes.

The following week a hollow-eyed woman in her mid-fifties appeared at the door of Elma's 'office.'

Elma recognised her at once and knew what the woman wanted. Respectfully, she waited until a harassed looking woman vacated the end cubicle before indicating it to her visitor, "It was that one" she said quietly and tactfully withdrew.

A small floral arrangement was later found resting on the cistern to mark a daughter's sorrow at her mother's passing.

On another occasion, a young woman had rushed into the room, rudely pushing aside some of the customers clustered around the mirror rearranging their hair. She plumped down hard on one of the chairs and it became quickly obvious to most of the ladies what the problem was when she began to groan and gasp, panting for air. "It's too soon," she had called out plaintively, "Help me please, the baby's coming."

What a day that was. It was talked of for years by Elma's regulars: the day a little boy first saw the light of day in Murrays' Ladies Room. "Lovely" was the consensus and several of the female witnesses were very happy to be there when the young woman brought the baby in a few weeks later to introduce him to Elma and thank her for the care she showed at such a difficult time. There had been some speculation that the boy might be named Murray, but this was decided against by his parents. Their effusive letter of thanks to the management team, along with their personal commendation of Elma, brought her to the attention of Mrs Pegram.

Mrs Pegram had long been aware that the junior

staff ladies' toilets, known colloquially, though regrettably, as the 'girls' bogs', left something to be desired. She had wondered how it could be improved and she suddenly hit on the woman for the job. Elma was summoned to Personnel. Mrs Pegram outlined the problem and made her suggestion:

"I wonder if you could cast a professional eye over the junior's loos and see if you could suggest any improvements. Economical improvements." she corrected herself, thinking of Mr McElvey's likely views on the matter.

"But what about my Ladies Room? Who will look after that?" Elma queried.

"Don't worry about that. This will only take a little of your time and I know you always have your Ladies Room in apple pie order." The two women paused slightly, trying to process this concept. Deciding that she knew what Mrs Pegram meant, Elma nodded. "I'll pop down when I can and make some notes."

"Terrific. No rush though." Mrs Pegram moved forward to shake Elma's hand as she ushered her out of the office.

Elma frowned to herself as she returned to her usual place of work.

Later that day, the post lunchtime rush over, Elma set off down the stairs to the basement where the Junior Ladies Room was located. As she pushed open the door, she was assailed by an overpowering smell of damp. The dim light revealed old, crazed tiles on the walls, clouded mirrors and a row of cracked, elderly sinks marked by tell-tale green trails from ever dripping taps. A single limp grey towel hung to one side. Taking a deep breath, she pushed open one of the cubicle doors and quickly closed it again. The various fittings had clearly been exemplary in their day, but that day was a very long time ago. Sighing, she looked around for somewhere to sit, but there was nothing.

What a truly dismal place, she thought.

Suddenly, from outside the door and far off, the sound of thundering footsteps echoed down the white tiled stairwell. A short while later, the door was pushed open, hitting Elma on the shoulder, and a dozen girls rushed in, diving towards the cubicles. A queue was formed by the late arrivals. Elma recognised some from various departments throughout the store. One of them looked at her curiously, "Are you one of the new girls then?" She enquired. Her friends chortled.

"No. I'm from the customers' Ladies Room on the second floor. Mrs Pegram asked me to see if I could recommend any improvements to this one." Elma replied severely.

"Gosh," the girl mused. "It would be brilliant if this could be improved." She indicated the room with a helpless gesture. A vacancy then appeared and she dived into the newly empty cubicle. Her comment was taken up by another girl in the queue.

"It's hard for us," she started. "The canteen is on the fifth floor and then we have to come all the way down here. We only have a fifteen-minute break in the mornings and afternoons, so sometimes we just have to choose." The others in the queue nodded in agreement. One took the argument further. "It's not healthy neither," she added accurately, if ungrammatically. Elma looked at the girls' tired faces and silently agreed. They must have to choose between the call of nature and a cup of tea. There could be no time for both.

With a banging of doors and a brief rinsing of hands in the cold water trickling from the taps, as quickly as they had arrived, the girls left. She could hear them clattering and panting up the many flights of stairs to their departments. Pausing only to check that all the taps were turned off as far as possible and all flushes were pulled (old habits die hard), she left the room and began the climb up to her natural habitat. She was relieved on entering the warmth, the kindly light and general air of calm that pervaded her Ladies Room. It was a haven. It was only a pity that the girls on the staff didn't have access to such a place on their hard-earned break. She knew they were not generally allowed to sit down at all and that, for many, the juniors' work consisted of a great deal of fetching and carrying. No wonder they looked so tired. She went to her little cupboard and sank down on her chair, pausing only to switch on her electric kettle. She always thought better after a cup of tea.

The next morning, she knocked at Mrs Pegram's door. On being called in, she entered and handed

Mrs Pegram a sheet of paper. On it she had listed what she felt was required to improve facilities for the girls. Mrs Pegram waved her to a seat and she sat down in some trepidation while Mrs Pegram scanned the list. Eventually, she looked up,

"Well you have given it all a lot of thought Mrs Struthers I must say." Her tone was not particularly encouraging. She continued, "I have to say, though, that it's most unlikely." She repeated, "Most unlikely, because I do not think this amount of expense would be sanctioned by the management." She shook her head sadly. "Is there not anything a bit, well, cheaper that could help?" she asked hopefully. "I just can't see Mr Mc-, I mean the management, agreeing to replace all the toilets, sinks and mirrors and redecorating the whole place, not to mention upgrading the lighting and heating. It can't be done, I'm afraid, but thanks for your input. I'll have a think." she said, dismissing her.

Elma left the room dejectedly and made her way back to her cupboard.

After a quick check that her Ladies Room, as she privately thought of it, was in good order, Elma grasped her mop and bucket, cleaning materials and polish and set off for the basement. At the very least I can give it a good clean, she thought, and set to scrubbing, bleaching and polishing with a will. Obviously the cleaners who were supposed to maintain this room made a very perfunctory job of it. They just don't care, Elma thought. In fact, nobody seems to care about these girls. If the management only gave some thought to it they'd have more energetic, enthusiastic junior staff with a lower staff turnover. She knew that the department heads often grumbled about the youngsters not being "stickers" in the way they had been. "They all want to go off and work in boutiques these days," one old timer had commented, to agreement all round.

As she cleaned and scrubbed, the retreating layers of grime began to reveal rather beautiful old tiles. She couldn't reach very far up the walls so the difference between newly scrubbed and 'au natural' tiles showed very clearly. She stood back and paused for thought. Ideas were forming in her head.

The next Monday, as the girls on first break rushed into the room, they halted, causing a domino effect to ripple back to those at the rear of the group. The room appeared to have been transformed overnight.

The glistening tiles stretched up to the ceiling and the effect was added to by the new light fittings that dangled down.

"Well, this place has certainly had a good scrub," said one.

"What on earth's come over the cleaner?" joked another.

"Same old mirrors and sinks though and, yes, toilets," said the first, pausing to check in one of the cubicles.

Entering the room as this was said, Elma felt a little disappointed that her handiwork, carried out in her own time, wasn't more appreciated. However, she stifled her dismay as she looked at the latest drooping new recruit to Handbags. She wasn't used to all the standing yet and was trying to perch on one of the sinks. It gave slightly with a sigh as the ancient piping came away from the wall. She sprang away from it with a gasp.

"Oh no. Sorry. What'll I do?" She asked looking around wildly, concerned that Elma had been a witness to this.

"Don't you worry," Elma reassured her. "It was bound to happen sooner or later."

Gratefully, the girl dived into a vacated cubicle and Elma gave the sinks a last polish before heading upstairs to start her shift.

Having decided to consult her brother-in-law, a plumber, about likely costs for replacement of the sinks and toilets, Elma sat down one evening to draw up costs. Even with a substantial discount, the final result was unlikely to be sanctioned by Mr McElvey. Elma sighed and drummed her fingers impatiently on the table top, staring at the figures as though trying to alter them by sheer force of will. No luck though. Her mind wandered frantically as she tried to think of a solution to the problem. She was feeling quite maternal towards the girls and really wanted to help.

Two months later, the management met to discuss an unusual turn of events. Mrs Pegram filled them in. "So after an inspection visit to the junior ladies' toilet a few months ago, I charged Elma Struthers, from the customers' Ladies Room," she added for the benefit of the men present who never had occasion to meet Elma. "Mrs Struthers is an excellent member of staff much praised by her ladies," she added to emphasise her value to Murrays. "Anyway, she found this, er facility," she said, in deference to Miss Murray's wincing at the word 'toilet'. "to be in poor order. Very poor order," she concluded heavily.

"In fact, it's no wonder the girls are leaving in droves. Why would they want to stay working in a place where there are such antediluvian expectations and conditions?"

Mr McElvey looked unimpressed. "Well, it was good enough for our older staff in their day. I don't know what's wrong with youngsters these days!"

"That attitude perhaps?" Miss Murray spoke at last. "We're struggling against the modern chain stores as it is. I gather that Marks and Spencer, for instance, have subsidised canteens, better pay and even a staff chiropodist to attend to sore feet from working on the shop floor. No antique, er, 'facilities' there."

Mr McElvey snorted.

"Why would anyone want to work here if they didn't have to?" she continued. "No. There's no doubt that we'll have to give some thought to upgrading staff conditions and, er, facilities."

She nodded appreciatively to Mrs Pegram.

"Actually," Mrs Pegram cleared her throat, "the

facilities seem to have improved themselves already."

"What do you mean?" Mr McElvey hissed suspiciously, "I haven't passed any invoices to be paid for improvements to facilities."

"I don't know how it's happened, but it just has," Mrs Pegram responded lamely.

"I think you'll need to tell us a bit more." Miss Murray said, intrigued.

Mrs Pegram started her story...

A short while later, a small deputation from the management floor made their way cautiously down the echoing staff stairs to the junior ladies' toilet. Mrs Pegram led Miss Murray and Mrs Carr, who had been deputised by Mr McElvey, to inspect the alleged improvements. It was between breaks so the toilet could be expected to be empty. Mrs Pegram pushed open the door.

"What do you think?"

Miss Murray didn't know quite what to say as she had never seen the place in its previous state. Certainly it looked quite nice. She said as much warily. They looked at the neat row of hand basins set in a vanity unit with a row of padded stools tucked beneath.

"Well it's a massive improvement as far as I can see," said Mrs Carr, pushing open a cubicle door to inspect it and nodding her approval. Everything was very much in order there it would seem. "I remember having to use these when I was a junior. It was pretty awful here even back then."

"I didn't know you started on the shop floor," Mrs Pegram looked at her with interest, but Miss Murray interrupted, "The fact of the matter is that there has been considerable upgrading here that we know nothing about. We don't know when, how, or by whom this was done. Louise, can you speak to the weekend caretaker?" Mrs Pegram nodded and Miss Murray continued "The workmen and this equipment must have been let in at some point. This isn't the work of the fairies!"

The small delegation made their way, panting slightly, up the stairs to the management corridor. Mrs Pegram went to her office to telephone the caretaker and also wondered if Mrs Struthers was worth talking to. She might have an idea as to the girls' mystery benefactor.

When the management team reconvened a few days later, all was revealed.

"It appears that Mrs Struthers herself funded this work," Mrs Pegram informed them.

"Good God! A member of staff?" Mr Philipson was horrified. "We can't have them paying for that sort of thing out of their own pockets. It's not right."

Mr McElvey was less sure. "We must be paying her far too much if she can afford that," he said.

"But how did she afford it?" Mr Soames was not a garrulous man.

"It seems she had a win on the Premium Bonds and all this came up while she was pondering what to do with the money. She told me that it didn't seem like her own money and when she heard we weren't likely to upgrade the toilets, she felt so sorry for the girls that she just went ahead and commissioned the work herself. I gather it was considerably less than we would have been charged for the work, but it was still a substantial amount."

Miss Murray sighed and sat back. "She must be reimbursed," she stated with a finality that even Mr McElvey recognised.

"Of course," Mrs Pegram agreed.

"Naturally," chorused Mr Philipson and Mr Soames. Mr McElvey said nothing.

"We'll need to find the right way to do it so she's reimbursed but is also recognised for her work far above and beyond the call of duty," Miss Murray mused.

"I've got an idea, leave it with me." Mrs Pegram could always be counted on to come up with a suitable scheme. They all nodded.

Next month as Elma was busying herself polishing the mirrors in the Ladies Room, a regular customer paused to chat as she brushed her hair. She glanced at Elma, then stood back to look at her directly.

"I say, what a magnificent brooch, or is it a badge," she asked, peering closely at the gold item pinned to Elma's overall.

"Oh," she replied modestly, "I got it for this." She indicated a framed certificate on the wall. It stated in beautiful calligraphy: *The Margaret Murray*

Award for Initiative by a Staff Member.

The customer looked impressed. "Well done you! You deserve it. I hope there was something more in it for you than a wee badge?"

"Yes," came the guarded reply. "There was a cash prize along with it." She blushed then whispered, "It was £10,000! Miss Murray's personal award."

"Gosh! What a wonderful sum. I hope you plan to do something exciting with it."

"Oh yes. I'm off to Canada in the summer to see my son and his family. There'll be a bit of money left over too, but I expect I'll manage to think up something to do with that too."

"Lovely!" The two ladies in the Ladies smiled at each other.

Chapter 5

A View from the Lodge

I'm Siri Joshi. I am twelve years old and I live at the lodge house next to the gate at Rosehill, Miss Murray's house. I haven't always lived here. I used to live in Africa in a country called Uganda. We had to leave there. I'm not sure why, but it was all a huge rush and we couldn't take much with us. I had to leave my precious cat behind. I try not to think of her because it makes me cry...

Sorry. I just thought of her again. I've stopped crying now. I hope the lady who promised to look after her really did. I know Daddy didn't trust her. "Too damned keen to move into our house and business," he said. He didn't know that my big sister Anjuli and I listened in on the adults' conversations. It was horrible knowing something awful was going to happen, but not being sure what it was. Anyway, something horrible did happen. We left in the middle of the night and drove and drove until we got to an airfield. Daddy left the car. We left everything really. All I remember of the flight was that it was cold. So cold. Good practice for when we got to Scotland I suppose. I'm a bit more used to it now but it's not really *comfortable* somehow. I don't think it ever will be, but it's better now I've got Scottish clothes, even if they are scratchy.

At first, we lived in a place called a Bed and Breakfast, but Daddy says that it was "extortionate" (whatever that means) and so we moved to a new place he found in the eaves of a big shop. It was very exciting living there. I loved it. Mummy hung the rugs up to make a little tent and we slept there quietly during the day. At night we could go out into the shop if we were careful and very, very quiet. It was fun there. Didn't last long though. One day a big bell rang and rang and we could hear people running downstairs. Mummy and Daddy were frantic. I'd never seen them so upset. Mummy shouted at Daddy, "We must go, it's not safe." Daddy said. "Nothing's safe. Nothing's ever going to be safe again." He was crying. I didn't know men cried. Luckily, Mummy took over and we ran down some stairs. Lots of people stared at us as we went out into a yard at the back. A lady gave me a sweetie though, so it wasn't all bad.

That was the start of things. That was when we met Miss Murray. She was kind to us. She still is. Now we live in a little cottage at the gate of her house. Everybody's happy. Daddy works in the big shop. He knows all about precious rugs, so it's ideal for him. Mummy helps Mrs Glen the housekeeper in the house. Mrs Glen is very old. She's very bossy too, but we sort of know she doesn't mean it and she's bossy to everyone, even Miss Murray. She's got a husband but he doesn't speak. Well, not much anyway. He's ancient too. Daddy helps him with the big lawn mower after work sometimes.

I go to school. It's better now. At first the other girls were mean to me and said nasty things. They called me 'Silly' instead of Siri and said I needed a wash as my skin was dirty. Why are people so nasty? Anyway, it all got sorted out when a big girl called Jennifer Hansen shouted at them one day and asked them how they would feel if they had to leave everything they knew and start again in a new country. Some of them even cried when she said that. Now they're my friends. Except horrible Vanessa. She's still a cow but, Jennifer says you get that. "She's pathetic really," and she's cool so she would know.

I like school. The teachers are kind (mostly) and I always try my best. I'm not the top of the class, but just doing OK is fine by me. I've discovered that I'm quite good at sport and I won lots of my races at the school sports day. I even won the high jump prize. What a surprise for Mummy and Daddy. The coach wants a word with me about extra training. Mummy wasn't keen, but Daddy says that we should take advantage of whatever opportunity arises. They had a bit of an argument about it. Mummy likes me and Anjuli to be at home as much as possible and tries to teach us Indian cooking. I don't know why. We're in Scotland now and I like the Scottish food. The school dinners are lovely. No one else likes them though. Odd. Mummy wants us to learn Indian dancing and Indian everything. She wants us to keep our Indian heritage she says. I didn't know we *were* Indian until we got here. I thought we were just *us*. Anyway, now I do geography, I know we came from Uganda, a place in Africa, not India. I tried to discuss this with Mummy, but she just sighed and said I don't understand. Maybe I will one day.

Daddy's happier now I think. He likes his work in the Carpet Department. Of course it's not his business like it was in the past, which he's sad about, but at least he's working with his precious rugs. His boss Mr Gavin just invited him on a buying trip so he's very pleased about that. "It's like a return to the old days," he told Mummy.

Apart from all the Indian stuff, I think Mummy likes working at Rosehill too. Mrs Glen is kind to her and they both seem to enjoy keeping the old furniture gleaming and everything nice for Miss Murray. How can anybody like cleaning though? Is this something that will come to me as I get older? I hope not!

I don't think Anjuli is very happy at the moment. There's big rows going on at home. She's very clever you see; her school work is brilliant (compared to mine anyway). Mummy and Daddy were so proud after they came home from parents' night at school. Apparently Anjuli could easily get into university. They even told Mr and Mrs Glen about it after they got home that night. We often pop over to the kitchen at Rosehill for cocoa after supper. It's cosy and sometimes they forget I'm there. I sit very quietly pretending to read a book and they talk away. Well, Mummy and Mrs Glen do. The men sit nodding. I sometimes think they're asleep with their eyes open. Anyway, that night they were all talking about Anjuli and Mummy and

Daddy were despairing about the cost of a university education when Miss Murray came in. She'd heard what they were saying and offered to cover the costs. Everyone was shocked. I'm not sure whether it was about the overhearing or the offer though: you should hear some of the things they say. Mummy went all red and Daddy nearly cried again, or at least he went all hoarse and coughed a lot. I'm getting worried about him. They all talked for ages, then noticed I was still there and they made a great fuss and we had to go back to the lodge. Anjuli wasn't there. She was at choir practice. Miss perfect Anjuli even has a lovely singing voice. Am I jealous? Yes, I think I am. Och, as they say here.

The rows started when Mummy and Daddy told her she could go to university as the school think she'd easily get in and Miss Murray had offered to pay. That was at breakfast. Anjuli went very quiet and said she'd have a think. We all looked at each other as she left the table. You'd think she'd be thrilled and want to snap it up. I expect it was the shock. However, it was us who had the shock when she got home from school that night and announced she didn't want to go to university. Well. What a scene! I found the shouting and crying upsetting so I sneaked away and sat in the rose garden until I thought things might have calmed down.

Mr Glen came too and sat on the bench next to me and smoked a pipe. He's very relaxing company. After a while, I told him what was happening at home.

He only nodded as though he'd suspected it all along, then sighed and said, "It's a sair fecht richt enough."

I don't know what that means, but I assume it's some sort of soothing Scottish saying. We sat for a while in comfortable silence before he finished his pipe and we both got up to return to our own kitchens. No Rosehill kitchen cocoa for me that night.

Since then the rows have seemed to go on night after night. Mummy is cross all the time and Anjuli doesn't say anything at all. She's not eating much and pushes her plate away from her as soon as they start on about the wonderful opportunity offered to her. I get myself to the rose garden every evening now. Sometimes Mr Glen is there too; sometimes it's just Bluebell the cat and me, but he's good company. I wonder what's going to happen. I wish everything could go back to how it was before. I tried to say that to Mummy, but she just shouted at me. She's not very happy. Daddy seems to spend less and less time at home too.

When I got home from school today Mummy was all smiles and had baked us a special cake. Very suspicious. When Daddy got home she said we should all sit down as she had something important to tell us. We all looked at each other. Well, at least she'd cheered up. Unfortunately, that was the calm before the storm, the worst ever storm! It turned out she'd been on the phone to our auntie in Birmingham and they'd come up with a grand new plan for Anjuli. She was to get married!

Apparently, Auntie Meenah knew just the right young man for her and she was currently in negotiations with his family on Mummy and Daddy's behalf. We were all too stunned to speak at first, then Daddy started to say something. He didn't look happy, but it was Anjuli's reaction that was most shocking. She stood up and just shouted at Mummy. I couldn't believe it! If I thought her reaction regarding university was bad, this was something in another league. The noise was awful. Mummy was loudly trying to describe the man's wonderful attributes as Anjuli shouted about how she couldn't believe her own mother would do a thing like that behind her back. She refused point blank to meet him. To ever meet him. It seemed to go on and on. Finally, Daddy stood up and roared, "Enough." He said he wanted to think about it and walked out. Mummy and Anjuli subsided into a very hostile silence and I slunk out. I just hoped Daddy hadn't gone to the rose garden. Thankfully, it was empty when I got there. I spotted Daddy sitting in the dark car as I passed by.

That night I heard Mummy and Daddy talking till late as Anjuli's muffled sobs kept me awake. I couldn't think what to say to her. Or to anyone. Things didn't get better. After a while people began to ask at school what was wrong with Anjuli and me. I got fed up with going home to stony silence, so one afternoon, after school, I just went straight to Mrs Glen's kitchen. She was knitting, but seemed pleased to see me. She made me some cocoa and gave me a lovely slice of cake. I was surprised how much I enjoyed it; I suppose I'd not had much appetite for ages. It's hard to be hungry in such a horrible, unhappy atmosphere. She watched me tucking in for a while, but when I sat back and wiped off the ring of cocoa around my mouth, she asked if I'd mind telling her what on earth was wrong with my mother. I suppose I should have expected this; I know how nosy she is. But she looked so kind and concerned that I couldn't hold back any more and burst into tears. I blurted out, "It's Anjuli."

"Oh no. Don't say she's ill!" Mrs Glen looked horrified. I told her it wasn't that, it was much worse. Then I poured out the whole story and then she poured out her side of the story too. Mummy and Daddy had stopped coming over for a chat after dinner and Mummy had been virtually silent as she worked in the big house. Mrs Glen had been sure they had done something wrong or said something to upset them. She was very relieved to hear that whatever had been wrong in the Joshi household was nothing to do with them. It's funny how people always think things must be their fault. I'd been feeling guilty too but didn't know why.

Anyway, we talked and talked and she gave me a wee cuddle, which somehow made me feel much better. Well, it was either that or the cake. Both were good. She tutted when I told her Mr Glen knew something was up but he must have forgotten to tell her about it. After a while I thought I'd better get home in case Mummy was worried about where I was. I thanked Mrs Glen and she gave me a sort of pat and said to leave everything with her.

That night after our silent supper there was a knock at the door. It was Mr Glen. He told Mummy and Daddy they were wanted over in the big kitchen. They sighed and Anjuli and I headed up to our rooms to start on our homework (or, in Anjuli's case, staring into space). Then Mr Glen said we were to come too. We were all pretty reluctant to follow this royal command to go to the big house but, of course, we set off at once.

To our surprise, Miss Murray was sitting in the kitchen with Mrs Glen. She got up when we came in and suggested we all sit around the table. She's very good at being in charge, although she actually looked pretty awkward and seemed to fumble around for words. Eventually she said that she and the Glens knew there was something badly wrong with the lodge family and they were all worried and wanted to help. Daddy started to talk, to fob her off I suppose, but Mummy interrupted and told her about the wonderful offer of marriage to the young man in Birmingham. Anjuli looked at the fireplace and sighed.

Miss Murray asked Anjuli what she thought about it and she blurted out that she wouldn't, couldn't even think about it and she and Mummy both burst into tears. Miss Murray and Mrs Glen looked at each other. Mr Glen put the kettle on.

Bluebell, who had been snuggled up against the Aga, tiptoed out and I wished I could follow him.

After a while, Miss Murray gently asked Anjuli what she herself actually wanted. She pointed out that the offer of university was still there and took it upon herself to say that no one could coerce Anjuli into marriage. Daddy drew himself up at that point, but Miss Murray just looked at him and said, "This is Scotland." We all looked at Anjuli.

She lifted her head up and looked directly at Miss Murray and said, "Thank you for asking me what I want."

She looked defiantly at Mummy and continued, "What I'd really like, what I really want to do is to start work in Murrays." She turned to look at Daddy, "I want to work like you, to specialise in something and to help customers and be friends with other girls and make money and just have, I don't know, fun!" She seemed to be on a roll. "I've worked and studied hard and done my best and I want a change from all that. I've got some great ideas how to help Murrays keep up to date and I just want the chance to do that. I think I've got something to offer Murrays."

She ran out of breath, but her eyes sparkled and she looked hopefully towards Miss Murray who nodded quickly.

"Well, Mr Joshi," she said. She was always very polite to him. "What do you think?"

Daddy seemed a little lost for words. He looked briefly at Mummy who had gone very quiet (and a bit red); she looked mutinous. Eventually, after a glance at Anjuli, he turned to Miss Murray, "Do you think you could find a place for Anjuli in the store Miss Murray? She's a bright girl and very hard working."

Mummy looked furious and seemed about to say something, but then shrugged and looked away.

Miss Murray was smiling, "Of course I can find a place for Anjuli. She's just the sort of girl we're always looking for. She's very young though. How about we start her as a junior and see how it goes? If she finds that large scale retail like ours is for her, in the long run there's no saying but we could sponsor her for further business studies and," she looked momentarily stern, "if, and I only say if, she's as good as I think she is, she could join the management training programme. She could have a great future at Murrays." She sat back. Mrs Glen put a cup of tea in front of her and nodded her approval. Well, after that everyone wanted to speak at once.

Anjuli was overjoyed, saying, "Yes, yes please."

Daddy looked very happy and Mrs Glen chuntered away to Mummy about the advantages of the scheme. Mummy began to nod reluctantly and finally said she'd better give Auntie Meenah a ring to tell her about the new developments.

So that was that. Anjuli finished her exams that term and left school. She started in Floristry and seems to be enjoying herself. Me next. I wonder what department I'll end up in? Must rush. Off to high jump practice.

Chapter 6

Resilience

I'm just on my way in to Murrays. It's my favourite shop by a mile. It feels like the gold standard for shops. I work there now (sort of) as it seems like the right place to be. The right thing to do. I've always done things right. I have. Really, I have. My mother always said I was the ideal baby; fed, slept, did everything just as she would have wanted. I was pretty too, everyone at the baby clinic said so. Then I walked early, started to talk, and said just the right things in just the right accent. I was always neat and tidy, my curls intact, even after a day at school, my white socks always pristine and resolutely up, never gathering at my ankles like the other girls'. I was Mummy and Daddy's pride and joy. I did well enough at school. I wasn't top of the class, but not near the bottom either. I gained reasonable grades in my exams and never embarrassed my parents at any social functions. Daddy said more than once that I never let them down.

After school I went to secretarial college. I'd rather have done something with flowers, but Mummy said secretaries meet all sorts of suitable people and I never argued with her. I never argued with anyone. She was right too. I did meet a suitable young man in my first job. Charles was a solicitor then. A young man very much on his way up. I was lucky to catch his eye when I did. We went out for a few wonderful months. He was made a partner in the law firm and to celebrate he took me out for a wonderful dinner and proposed. I can't say it was very romantic really. He just took my hand and said, "The senior partner says that a solicitor in my position should be married. It gives clients more confidence if they feel they're dealing with a family man, so how about it?" I was a bit flustered. I wasn't sure if he'd discussed it with Daddy, but, sure enough, it turned out he had. Daddy had agreed (and also agreed to set us up in a nice bungalow in the suburbs, but I didn't know that at the time).

After that things moved fast. Mummy and I had a marvellous time planning the wedding. I hardly saw Charles as he was working so much, although he took great interest in the guest list, which was surprising as he didn't want to invite many guests from his side of the family.

The wedding itself was lovely. I'll never forget it. It was the best day of my life. I felt like a princess as I drifted up the aisle on Charles's arm on our way to a sumptuous (and very expensive) reception in the best hotel. Daddy had done us proud.

Daddy had done us proud with our new house too. I'd anticipated spending time with Mummy after the wedding, planning how to decorate and furnish it, but Charles said it was none of her business: it was our home and we were to furnish it as we wanted. By this he meant as he wanted. I don't know when it first struck me that he wasn't really the charming person we'd all thought. I had dismissed the comments about him from the other secretaries. I'd thought they were just jealous that I, the newest recruit, was waltzing off with the handsome new partner. He was very handsome then and that sort of thing mattered to me then. Not so much now.

Charles said I wasn't allowed to work after we were married. This made me feel special somehow. A bit smug I suppose. However, I became a tad bored after I'd done everything I possibly could to our home and garden: everything washed, ironed, hoovered, dusted, polished and tidied. I shouldn't have mentioned it to Charles though. What happened was my own fault and only to be expected. He was tired and out of sorts after a long day. I resolved to put it behind me and forget about it. I didn't go out for a few days after that, then it was sunny so I could wear my large sunglasses. Least said soonest mended, as Mummy always said.

Luckily, I was a good cook and Charles soon began to ask clients home for dinner. I had looked forward to presiding over dinner parties and being admired for my hostessing skills. I was a bit surprised at the sort of guests he invited though. I expected young professionals like ourselves, but they were older and a bit seedy really. Sometimes they had wives with them or girlfriends. Sometimes they came on their own. After dinner, rather than have pleasant chats over coffee and port, Charles would take them off to his study. I'd hear them talking and laughing. The whole house used to stink of cigar smoke for days afterwards. I just cleared up and washed the dishes. That was my job apparently.

Two children came along in time: a boy and a girl. Mummy and Daddy would have been so happy to have grandchildren, but, tragically, both my parents were killed outright in a car accident on their first ever holiday to the continent. At the time I thought I'd never recover from the loss. I cried for days and days. I was inconsolable. And of course, Charles did nothing to console me. He gave me two days to snap out of it, then all he wanted to know about was their will. Turns out that Mummy and Daddy had the measure of him after all and their entire estate was left in trust to me as their only child; he couldn't touch the capital. He touched me then alright. There was nobody to notice by now though, except the dentist, who foolishly wondered about my loose and missing teeth. He restored them beautifully, then I had to change dentist. Charles insisted.

Linda and Peter, the children, were little chips off the old block. Just like Charles they both were. Linda was beautiful and completely spoilt by her father. He could deny her nothing. Any time I tried to establish behavioural boundaries he ignored them and encouraged her to ignore them as well. She soon became a complete brat and the despair of her teachers (and me). Peter in his turn was a very handsome boy. A handsome boy with some very ugly habits. I was forever being asked to see his head teacher about his bullying. He was downright cruel. Our neighbours didn't have much to do with us, but

I was mortified one day when they arrived at my door with their dead pet rabbit that Peter had apparently tortured. I believed them. Charles didn't and stormed round to their house. I don't know what he said. They moved soon after. The other neighbours avoided us.

The dinner parties continued. By now I just prepared and served the food. I didn't have to act as hostess at all. Yvonne, Charles's secretary, often came to these dinners. I did resent the way she ordered me about and her overfamiliarity with my husband. I spoke to him about it once but he 'put me in my place' as he called it. I left it at that. Anything for a quiet life.

We did have a 'nice' life. We went on holidays to expensive resorts, the children went to the right schools (according to Charles) and I was always nicely turned out. I tried to be polite to anyone I met, but tended to discourage any friendly overtures, pleasantly turning down any invitations to coffee mornings or ladies' afternoon teas. I sometimes overheard people talking about me and commenting on how stand-offish I was. If only they knew. I longed for a friendly group to confide in but had to confine myself to Charles, the children and people he thought were suitable company: not that I was allowed to talk much.

My only other social outlet was shopping. I loved shopping. Not only for the undeniable joy of acquiring new things, but for the brief chats with helpful shop assistants. Snippets of meaningless but pleasant conversation. The nicest of these were in Murrays of course. What a pleasure it was to wander from department to department. I often thought they must have a policy of only employing nice people. I did have some especial favourites though, which led me to make some unwise purchases. Unwise only in the price I had to pay back home when Charles saw the bills. It was almost worth it though for the little flash of interest I saw in the face of one assistant as she listened to me tell her about my holiday, or another telling me about her mother's latest illness. A little laugh in recognition of a small shared joke began to mean such a lot to me. I'd love to have been allowed to work in Murrays myself then.

I sometimes wondered what my parents would have said about my life and how it turned out. I was still doing everything right and correctly though. I hoped they would still be proud of me.

Of course this was before the time of 'the great shame' as I call it. Charles was disbarred from the law. Struck off. Not allowed to practise law ever again. Not that what he'd been practising was, strictly speaking, legal anyway. He'd been defrauding clients, including my parents' trust, and was left owing hundreds of thousands of pounds. It was all gone. High stakes gambling apparently. It's an illness. Apparently. I was left with a husband in prison, two out of control children and absolutely no money. I'm ashamed to say that my first thought was thank goodness my parents aren't alive to see this. My second thought was, hooray, Charles will be away for years. It was only then that I thought, oh my God, what will I do now?

Unbelievably, and luckily as it turned out, Daddy had registered the bungalow in my name only, so it couldn't be seized as an asset. Charles had slipped up there. At least we had a roof over our heads. The children had to leave their private schools of course. If they had been less troublesome or even slightly nicer children it's possible the schools might have helped out with bursaries, but there was no chance of that in their cases. In fact, there was a definite air of 'good riddance' at the end of my painful interview with Peter's headmaster. I didn't blame them. Both the children, by now awkward teenagers, would have been too embarrassed to face their schoolmates anyway after the extensive newspaper coverage of their father's exploits.

Charles's secretary, Yvonne, had attended court each day looking very glamorous and was much photographed as his 'wife.' She came to the house one evening to collect some jewellery (my wedding pearls) that she'd allegedly been promised by Charles. She got short shrift I can tell you. I quite enjoyed it. It was the first time I've ever really given vent to my feelings. As I shouted, "Get lost you money-grubbing slag," to her rapidly retreating figure, I felt something give inside me. Something changed. God, it felt great. Better than that, it felt right. I was doing absolutely the right thing. I nodded briefly to the neighbours that I glimpsed peeping out from behind their curtains to see what the disturbance was and I turned and closed the front door.

With my newfound resolution, I summoned the children to the dining room and told them to sit down. Blinking in surprise at being ordered to do something by their doormat mother, they opened their mouths to protest, but I silenced them with my first few words.

"Right you two, things have to change around here. Your precious father is no better than a criminal and his gambling has left us destitute." I eyed them beadily. "Absolutely destitute. There. Is. No. Money!"

They demurred, but I continued. "Here is the plan: I sell this house, invest the capital raised for income and with that income we rent a small cheap flat nearer town. Nearer town because you two are not going back to school."

Their faces brightened, but only momentarily. "You're both going to have to get jobs. You'll have to work for a living."

Quelling their protests, I set them to tidying the house before the estate agent came to value the property. I think they were so shell shocked by everything that they went along with my orders. This had never happened before and I revelled in the feeling of control I had never had in the past.

Things moved fast after that. It was a lovely house in a pleasant location. In a way I was sad to lose it. It was my last link with Mummy and Daddy, but I thanked Daddy's foresight in leaving me something of my own. It was only a pity that Charles had fraudulently broken the trust fund they left me by forging my signature.

We moved onwards and downwards. The affordable flat I found was tiny. Linda and I shared a bedroom and Peter slept on the couch in the sitting room. Most of our good furniture and possessions had been sold to add to the capital sum which kept us more or less.

The obvious place for Peter and Linda to find work was Murrays. Neither of them had achieved any qualifications and their expensive education seemed to have passed them by completely, but they looked and sounded presentable. They completed application forms and were duly interviewed and offered employment. The rates of pay and conditions of employment seemed to come as a nasty surprise, but it was time my children learned the value of work.

Linda was a very pretty girl and was immediately placed in Cosmetics and Perfumery. To my surprise, she seemed to like it there. She enjoyed being made up to give the other girls practice and often came home looking quite ridiculous: plastered in improbable make-up and with unfeasibly long false eyelashes weighing her eyelids down. She developed a good sales manner and gradually built up a reputation as a make-up artist herself. The long hours standing behind the counter in the stuffy atmosphere was tiring for her and she was glad to slump down on the sofa at the end of her working day. She even seemed to appreciate the meals I produced for us in the little kitchenette.

Things were harder for Peter, but ultimately much better. He was placed with the porters unloading deliveries and transporting goods around the store. It was hard physical work, something he had no experience of. The other porters made a fool of his accent and his attempts at laziness. When he was caught bullying and intimidating a man with mild learning disabilities in the packing department, he was beaten black and blue by his colleagues and, to his outrage, absolutely no witnesses came forward. Mrs Pegram in Personnel explained this to me over an apologetic telephone call. I don't suppose she realised I was more accustomed to being informed of Peter having hurt others than being the victim himself. I graciously accepted her apologies and assurance that this was an extremely rare occurrence in Murrays.

The chastened Peter resumed his duties with a newfound diligence. He was aware of the awkwardness of course and tried to avoid the others at breaks. However, they were a good-natured bunch and gradually their banter broke through his cautious reserve. Before long he was playing football with them in the delivery yard during breaks. He was asked to join the store five-a-side football team and began to travel with them for matches on their days off.

Such changes. Such a new life. I never visited

Charles or informed him of our new address. I expect he'll be out soon and I really don't want to see him. I suppose he'll eventually track us down. We've discussed what we might do in that event. It's nice being able to discuss things with Linda and Peter. Nice being treated as an equal, or even someone worthy of respect. They don't want anything to do with him either.

Nowadays I work at Murrays too. It's not exactly a paid job, well not paid by Murrays anyway, or only indirectly. I've always liked shopping. I love the beautiful things they sell in Murrays. I can't afford their prices of course, but I still acquire them. No one suspects that such a respectable lady could possibly be stealing. I have a list of my own 'customers' now and fulfil their requirements to order efficiently and economically. It's amazing how much I can make from a Hermes scarf or a Ciro pearl necklace for example. Murrays must be making a large profit. Of course, unlike them, my overheads are, well, zero (unless you count my bus fares). My friends throughout the various departments would be amazed at what I seem able to whisk away. I'm very good at it. You could almost say it's a talent of mine. It's nice to have my own business and to be in charge of my own destiny at last.

I do feel guilty of course, but needs must when the devil drives, or Charles as I call him.

Chapter 7

Speculators

The Tea Room on the third floor was as popular as ever with a certain group of Edinburgh ladies. These ladies eschewed the chrome and bright colours of the first floor 'Caffe Fino' in favour of their somewhat shabby favourite meeting place. They had been meeting every Friday for coffee and scones for longer than they could remember. As staff came and went, the Friday ladies seemed a permanent fixture. Their numbers were sadly depleted now due to the unfortunate demise of Noreen. This had been followed by a brief but successful career attending strangers' funerals, which the ladies had all enjoyed – particularly the post-funeral refreshments. However, this activity was curtailed by the discovery that they were not the only group of ladies involved in that somewhat disreputable activity.

One particular spring Friday, Helen, the most forceful of them, sat back in her chair and sighed. "What is it dear?" asked Sandra, a very smart-looking person.

"I'm just sick of it all." Helen sighed again. Sandra and Irene exchanged worried glances. This wasn't like Helen at all. They regarded her as their leader.

Irene solicitously enquired, "Sick of what exactly? Your scone?" Irene cared a great deal about the quality of scones and, indeed, all types of food.

"No. No, it's not," Helen responded impatiently, leaning forward. "I'm just fed up of being hard up. Of all this penny pinching. And I fancy a change of scene. I'm sick of this place. Sick of the town. Of just everything," she said defiantly before subsiding back in her chair again.

Sandra and Irene had never heard her talk like this. They were worried. "What's happened?" asked Sandra kindly.

Helen sighed again.

"I think it's just all this royal wedding stuff."

"But we love hearing about the royal wedding. We've been looking forward to it for months." Irene struggled to understand her friend's problem.

"I know. I know. It's just…" Helen glared at them fiercely, "it's just that I'd really, really like to go and see it but I can't. I can't at all."

"I know," agreed Irene miserably. "We can all watch it together at my place if you like?" she said, brightening visibly. "We could have champagne and strawberries and smoked salmon sandwiches and…" Her happy list of delicious treats was interrupted by Helen glumly saying, "As if we could afford champagne worth drinking."

"Maybe if we saved up?" said Sandra, ever the peacemaker.

"Well, we'll just have to, won't we?" replied Helen resignedly. She continued. "All the fuss about the royal wedding has got me thinking. It's years and years since I was in London. I'd love to see it again, particularly en fête, all decorated and everyone happy for a change." She looked at them all. "I want to see Charles and Diana in their carriage driving down the Mall. I want to be part of it all somehow."

"My sister-in-law in Barnes has said I can stay any time. She's got a huge house. My brother did very well," Sandra added smugly. Irene gave her a look.

"Don't suppose she'd want three of us though…?" Helen sensed an opportunity.

"I could ask. I'm sure it would be OK with her. She's on her own now the children are married. Actually, I don't know why she doesn't move somewhere more convenient…" Sandra started off on a topic the others had heard many times before.

Helen interrupted. "But that doesn't help with the rail fares and day to day expenses. I bet the prices will rocket around that time." They all agreed. Caution was thrown to the wind and another pot of tea was ordered. The ladies had a thorny problem to work on.

Irene, thinking mainly of meals, wondered how long would they be there for? "Three days? That's three dinners and lunches. Could be pricy. I expect we would be given breakfasts at your sister-in-law's?" she added hopefully.

"I'm sure Thelma would provide breakfast. We'd need to give her a nice present or take her out for a meal of course."

"Of course," they all nodded. Irene wondered if they went in for street parties in Thelma's area of London.

"It's the rail fares that could snooker us." Helen brought them back down to earth. "There's no doubt that we'd need fairly serious money to get us to London for the royal wedding."

"Well we could each put up a bit I expect. I know I'd be willing to dip into my savings for a one-off like this," said Sandra optimistically.

"Me too," added Irene, and Helen said she could do about £50. If they all put up £50 then they would have about half of what they needed for the trip to London. Gloomily, they considered their options.

"Where can we beg borrow or steal another £100?" Helen wondered. "I can't ask the family. They're hard put getting the children everything they need for school and paying their own bills." The others' families were in a similar position.

"Where do people get money?" the question was posed. "Working? But we're all retired and even if we did work it would take ages at our hourly rates even if anyone would take us on." said Irene, answering her own question.

"What we need is some sort of windfall. Does anyone have any Premium Bonds?" asked Sandra. "Or do the pools?"

"We can't count on winning on those though." Helen put paid to that suggestion. "It's like gambling. My Jimmy always said that only the bookies win on that."

They all agreed. With sighs all round they gathered up their belongings and, with a wave to the counter staff, left the tea room, each pondering the knotty financial problem.

The next week Helen arrived early and waved the others over to their table impatiently. Once they were settled, teas poured and scones at the ready, she leaned forward confidentially.

"I have it," she said in triumph.

"Have what?" Irene asked, looking doubtfully at her scone. Surely they had shrunk recently?

"I have worked out how we can raise the rest of the money for our trip to London," Helen answered.

"Oooh, do tell," urged Sandra.

"Well," started Helen, looking cautiously around her for fear of listeners. The ladies themselves were keen eavesdroppers. "It was the mention of bookies that got me thinking."

"We can't be bookies; you surely don't mean that!" said Irene.

"Well, no, not exactly," Helen explained, "I just wondered if we couldn't run a book on the Grand National."

"What!" Sandra squeaked.

Others turned their heads at the sound of her raised voice. "Sorry," she whispered. "But you'd better explain."

"It's like this, we 'sell' tickets for the horses and the one who holds the ticket for the winning horse gets the prize money."

"How do we make money out of that unless one of us buys the winning ticket?"

"That's the beauty of it," Helen continued, "If we sell each ticket for say £5 and there's forty runners in the race," she said, proudly displaying her very recently acquired knowledge of horse racing terminology, "That's £200. The prize could be £100 so we'd make £100 ourselves. There would be work to do and some expenses so it's quite a reasonable percentage to keep back."

"One of us might even hold the winning ticket," Irene was excited at the prospect.

"There's a chance, like any other. Each of us can buy as many tickets as we like of course. Our main problem might be selling the tickets in the first place. I don't know about you ladies but my circle of contacts has reduced a lot since I retired."

"Good point. But I'd buy two so that's a start." said Irene, throwing caution to the wind.

"Me too," chipped in Sandra.

"There's a bit of work to do. The race is in April so we've got six weeks. I'll find out the horses' names and type out tickets."

Helen was as good as her word and the next week she turned up with a neatly typed list of horses entered for the race. The ladies scanned the list doubtfully.

"This is hard. I just don't know which one I'd go for," said Sandra.

"They all sound nice," Irene offered.

"Well I've been studying the 'form' and as far as I can see you might as well just have a lucky dip,"

Helen put in. The ladies stared at the list uncertainly.

"I think 'Royal Exile' and 'Royal Stuart' sound like nice horses. I was always interested in history." Helen continued.

"'My Friendly Cousin' could be a good omen?" Sandra suggested. "And I'll go for a horse with an Irish sounding name. That will be lucky. How about 'Bryan Boru'? I wonder what colour he is," she pondered.

Irene wasn't so sure. "I'll go for The Vintner, I do like a nice glass of wine, and, oh, I don't know," she waved her buttery knife over the list and landed its greasy tip on Aldaniti. "That's me chosen," she concluded.

Helen sighed and brushed off the greasy mark. "Right then. That's six horses off the list and thirty four more tickets left to sell. Who to, though? That's the problem."

The ladies ruminated. Just then, Alan, the manager of the Tea Room and a great friend of the ladies, wandered towards their table. Helen scrambled the papers away into her handbag as he approached.

Spotting this, Alan felt slightly miffed.

"OK. What are you hiding from me girls?" he queried.

"Nothing," said Helen defensively.

"Aw come on. I'm not daft. What's up?" He drew up a seat and joined them, waving over to the counter staff to bring him a pot of coffee. After it was brought over to the table, Irene signalled to Helen to show him the list.

"What's this then?" He scanned the list, noting the ladies' names after the horses of their choice.

"Well it's like this," Sandra started, but Helen cut in,

"We're fundraising to help send three old ladies to London to see the royal wedding. We're selling tickets for each horse in the Grand National and giving half the total money raised to the winning ticket holder."

"What's left over should be enough to get us all to London." Irene confirmed his suspicion as to who the old ladies were.

Sensing a good opportunity, Helen asked brightly, "Would you like to buy a ticket? They're £5 each?"

"£5? That's an awful lot," he ventured cautiously; he was anxious not to hurt the ladies' feelings.

"Well there are expenses involved in running something like this and it *is* for a good cause," Irene pleaded.

"Alan," Helen said portentously, "We all know that one has to speculate to accumulate." He thought about it. After all, he'd recently had a nice pay rise.

"OK then, I'll take one." He scanned the list and chose Delmoss at random.

"Now, do you know anyone else who'd like one?" queried Sandra.

"Or two," added Helen hopefully.

Alan thought for a while, then suggested that the porters generally liked a bit of a punt. He agreed to approach them on the subject.

The ladies thought about their various 'contacts' and resolved to try to confine sales to Murrays itself as it might be easier to keep control this way, rather than selling to a variety of friends, neighbours and families, all of whom might disapprove. All of them most certainly *would* disapprove, as they were all well aware. With Alan on their side, they should be relatively successful in the venture. Each of them had pet departments at Murrays where they were familiar and popular customers. It was possible they could each make some sales there.

Alan was as good as his word. The porters all signed up for tickets and various horses were chosen. Jim and the lads there were very enthusiastic and invited interested parties, as they put it, to join them in the porters' lodge to watch the race on their illicitly stored portable TV. This was duly noted by the ladies. Meanwhile, Helen successfully sold tickets to her friends in Hosiery, Fancy Goods and Notions and Ladies Outdoor garments. Irene struck lucky in the Food Hall, as might be expected, as well as in the Outsize Department. Sandra, at the expense of a new hairdo and facial, sold several tickets in the Hair and Beauty salon, as well as Soft Furnishings. The number of tickets to sell diminished satisfactorily until there were only a very few left. They decided to traverse the shop nonchalantly striking up conversation with staff as they went and, if at all possible, casually introducing the topic of the Grand National and their charitable effort on behalf of the three old ladies.

This worked well, several were snapped up in China and Glass and the remaining ones in Carpets and Rugs and the Handbag Department. Ladies Shoes sniffily dismissed them, as did the staff in Menswear (who had already heavily invested in the outcome of the Grand National at the local bookmakers). Finally, they were all sold. Helen banked the £200 and they eagerly awaited the great day. The plan had worked perfectly.

The day dawned at last. Helen was aware of an unaccustomed feeling of nervousness, a quivering feeling in her stomach. Is this why they call it a "flutter on the horses" she asked herself as she cleaned her teeth that morning. Sandra, meanwhile, was wondering what the accepted dress style was for an afternoon at a porters' lodge. Irene packed a picnic for them all as they were sure to be hungry during all the excitement of the race.

The small group assembled around the old television set in the porters' lodge. The ladies had been ceremoniously ushered to an extremely elderly and disreputable sofa and had gingerly taken their seats, swaying gently towards the middle as the springs gave way under the unaccustomed weight. Others, who had escaped from various departments, perched on trolleys or upturned boxes as best they could to catch a glimpse of the flickering picture. Excitement filled the tiny space. At last they were off! The group groaned as, one by one, the various horses refused, unseated their riders, or worse, fell. Irene was mortified when The Vintner refused at an open ditch.

"Well really, I didn't think he'd be such a coward," she said in disgust.

Alan was similarly disappointed when Delmoss fell. "But at least he tried," he concluded, looking darkly at Sandra whose horse, "My Friendly Cousin" had just pulled up and refused to ride on. She looked down blushing with annoyance.

"How embarrassing," she muttered as the dangerous race continued, shedding horse after horse until only Helen and Irene had a potential winner still running. Royal Exile and Aldaniti galloped on. Helen's Royal Exile began to fall back as Aldaniti and Spartan Missile pulled ahead of the remaining horses. It was neck and neck until Aldaniti, in a last great burst of energy, spurred on by his jockey, Bob Champion, was triumphant. Irene nearly passed out with excitement, her heart beating what felt like double time.

"Oh my, oh my. I've won," she said over and over again.

Looking at her sourly as he tore up his ticket Jim muttered, "You'd think she'd been riding the bloody thing herself." His friends nodded.

In the excitement of it all, they had been making a very great deal of noise. This had echoed up the staff staircase and, most unfortunately, attracted the attention of Barry Hughes. He puffed his way down to the basement and burst into the porters' lodge just as an ugly dispute broke out.

"How can it be a swizz if Irene won?" Helen demanded, "No one could predict the outcome of the race."

"Well it's just not right that one of the organisers won all that money," Jim muttered.

"Won all what money?" demanded Barry. There was a gasp and a general shuffling towards the door by the unlucky punters. "What's going on," he asked again in a quieter tone, noting the presence of the three lady customers. Helen swept as authoritatively to her feet as the sagging sofa allowed.

"Just a little charitable event," she informed him airily.

"I think you might have to tell me a bit more about this 'event,'" Barry said heavily. "I think we should discuss this upstairs don't you?"

Upstairs in the boardroom, Miss Murray looked at them and groaned, "Ladies, ladies what were you thinking?"

"We were just trying to raise some money to pay our rail fare to London for the royal wedding." Helen answered defensively. Sandra and Irene nodded vehemently.

"We're just old pensioners," Irene put in pitifully, "We want to see the Queen one last time." An incipient tear, noticed by Mrs Pegram, trembled in her eye.

"Well, you see it was gambling ladies," Miss Murray explained kindly. "We can't condone such an illegal activity on our premises."

"I didn't think. We just didn't think." Sandra said. She looked up at them, "What are you going to do?"

"I'm not actually sure." Miss Murray was flummoxed. In all her time at the helm of the business she'd never, in point of fact, faced such a situation. Barry looked on sternly. He was desperate to call the police. He looked forward to liaising with his former colleagues about the illegal gambling den that he, Barry, had uncovered.

There was silence as they all pondered the next step. To their surprise, there was a knock at the door and Mrs Carr, the secretary, entered. "I wonder if I might have a word?" she asked Miss Murray.

"Later perhaps Mrs Carr, we're a bit taken up with these ladies just now."

"Actually, it was in relation to this, er, situation that I wanted to speak to you. Perhaps outside?"

With a short nod, Miss Murray got up and indicated that Mrs Pegram should accompany her to the corridor. They shut the door behind them leaving the quailing ladies under the unsympathetic eye of Barry.

In the corridor they looked expectantly at Mrs Carr. "It's like this," she explained and outlined a potential course of action open to Miss Murray. It was a topic with which she was unexpectedly familiar. The management ladies looked at each other and at Mrs Carr and nodded. Miss Murray smiled, "Thank you Mrs Carr. You just might have saved the day." Mrs Carr dipped her head self-deprecatingly.

Ten long minutes later Miss Murray and Mrs Pegram re-entered the room, Mrs Pegram struggling to suppress a smile.

"Right," began Miss Murray fixing the three ladies with a look, "I now gather that what you have been doing is running a charity workplace sweepstake. Quite legal within a workplace *if* held for the benefit of employees."

"But we're not..." burst out Irene. Mrs Pegram moved forward with a sheaf of papers and gave out one to each. They looked down at them eagerly. After reading hers, Helen looked up smiling.

"Temporary contracts?"

"Yes, I see no reason why you shouldn't be employed on an extremely short-term basis consisting of, actually, just today. Then you would technically be staff and your activity quite legal," Miss Murray said with more confidence than she really felt.

Barry glowered. The date on the contracts matched the day of the 'sweepstake,' so they were theoretically watertight but it probably should not be examined too closely. However, they were only old ladies who wanted to see the royal wedding. It was unlikely that any Procurator Fiscal would do other than dismiss such a case if brought before them. Barry was unwilling to collude in such a cover up, but, equally, he didn't want to show himself in a negative light in front of Mrs Pegram.

"Well, if they are staff, what work are they going to do?" he asked. "Even if it's only for the rest of the day." That set them thinking. There wasn't much time left until the shop closed. Seeing a way out of their troubles, Helen eagerly called out, "We'll do anything, anything at all." Mrs Pegram nodded.

A short while later a telephone call was put through to the Tea Room. The manager was alerted to the impending arrival of three 'mystery shoppers' who would be coming to test the quality of the afternoon tea. The works were to be provided: sandwiches, scones and cake were to be scrutinised and a written report submitted. Miss Murray valued her elderly customers and had been highly amused by their enterprise, but she couldn't let her sympathies show in front of Barry and the other staff.

Later, upstairs in the Tea Room, quite overwhelmed by both the events of the day and the unaccustomed quantity of provender in front of them, the ladies sat in silence. Suddenly, an irrepressible bubble of laughter emerged from Irene. She couldn't help herself.

"We're going to London to see the Queen, here we go, here we go, here we go!"

Helen frowned, but couldn't quite prevent a smile breaking out.

Sandra joined in and proposed a most unlikely

toast in tea

"Here's to us, wha's like us."

The others grinned and joined in, adding in a very unladylike way, "Damned few, and they're a' deid!"

Chapter 8

A Fine Romance?

Susan Harrison, the new girl in Hosiery, was an extraordinarily quiet, self-effacing young woman. Looking at her, Mrs Garland, Hosiery's Head of Department, sometimes wondered whether she'd done the right thing in accepting her as their new junior. Not that there was any real choice, but Mrs Pegram liked to let the senior staff think they had a say in these things. Unarguably though, it suited Mrs Garland, a plump, bustling lady in her early fifties, to have a virtually silent "yes person" in her department.

Mrs Garland was accustomed to being in charge of any and every interaction, both social and business related. She did the talking and woe betide anyone rash enough to think otherwise. She steamrollered her way through sales and there were many ladies who left her department the bemused owners of stockings or other unmentionables in sizes and hues at some variance from those they set out to purchase. Mrs Garland had stock to shift and shift it she would. Ladies wanting to buy up to date patterned tights or pantyhose in the latest colours would leave with fully fashioned, seamless, run-proof stockings in colours such as Grecian Gold or Hawaiian Haze. The 1950s and 60s had been Mrs Garland's heyday and she saw no reason to update what she sold. The wonder was that customers returned. As styles moved on in other departments to reflect the 1980s, regulars seemed to hope that somehow Hosiery would too. No such luck.

Hosiery was conveniently located next to Ladies Lingerie and customers had to walk through Hosiery to get to Lingerie. Thus, it occupied a funnel-like space between the main staircase and the exotic haven of Lingerie, aka ladies' underwear. Hosiery was low ceilinged and, with its thick, mushroom-coloured carpet, warm beige walls and discreet lighting, it formed a luxurious haven. The various display units were placed around the walls and, in a few places, alarmingly disembodied legs displayed a range of stockings of varying style and hue. The sales desk was angled away from any enquiring glances from passers-by and a dainty little chair was placed by the glass-topped desk for weary customers to flop down on if required.

As the route to Lingerie, Hosiery's location offered Mrs Garland the perfect opportunity to seize upon transiting customers and set her powerful sales technique in motion. The startled expression of her victims was a great source of amusement to the staff from Lingerie as they observed customers trying to run the gauntlet through Hosiery.

Unlikely though it may seem, Susan took to Mrs Garland from the first time she met her. It must have been something to do with the contrast between Susan's family and life experience so far and the vibrant, forceful Mrs Garland. Susan was a conspicuously unassertive girl from an exceptionally quiet family. She was the only child in her generation and her pale aunts, silent uncles and morose father's and mother's voices seldom rose above a whisper. She was accustomed to a life of quiet endurance and it was expected that she would reflect this upbringing in her own manner. Thus, for Susan, Mrs Garland exploded into her life like a huge firework. She was dazzled by her and watched her constantly. She marvelled at Mrs Garland's way with customers and how she managed the buyer, as well as any members of management who dared to make suggestions regarding how she run her department. Susan revelled in learning all about the stock and if Mrs Garland liked it, then so would Susan.

"Who would believe there was so much to stockings and tights?" she breathed to her parents one evening over their hushed evening meal. Her parents nodded appreciatively, her mother's eyebrows raised with interest. They were inaudibly glad that their daughter was happy in her work.

It was soon noted that Susan seemed to hover near Mrs Garland at all times. "Like a small moon orbiting planet Garland," commented the poetic Mrs Jackson, Senior Sales in Lingerie.

"More like a wee boat in tow," replied the other, less whimsical Lingerie Assistant. They laughed as they heard the redoubtable Mrs Garland utter her most frequently used phrase, "Not now, Susan."

This phrase was uttered by Mrs Garland hundreds of times a day. In fact, almost any time

Susan began to speak she was silenced in this way. Susan didn't mind at all. She thought it extremely unlikely that anything she had to say would be of interest or relevance to Mrs Garland. It was sometimes unfortunate for Mrs Garland that she did ignore her, otherwise she might have been alerted to the theft of a large box of "lightweight, bend-easy, micromesh elasticated stockings," by a sinister-looking woman wearing a capacious overcoat.

On another occasion, Susan was unable to interrupt the flow of Mrs Garland's conversation with Jim the Porter to point out that four customers were irritably waiting for her to finish discussing his departmental shortcomings.

She was heard to say, "Not now, Susan," so often that this became poor Miss Harrison's nickname and it was widely used throughout the store.

Although Susan loved her work in Hosiery and she loved Murrays itself in a general way, there were aspects of her daily routine that she was less keen on. Downright unhappy would be a more apt way of describing her feelings on the matter of breaks and lunches. She wasn't sure if this was because in a two-person department it wasn't possible for them both to be away at the same time, so she was separated from Mrs Garland for these breaks. It could also have something to do with her shyness, making it hard for her to face the cheerful, noisy camaraderie of the Junior Staff Ladies Room or the smoky, intimidating canteen atmosphere. There was no doubt that she had a real problem with breaks. At first she tried to pretend she'd forgotten to take her break, then she'd say she didn't need a break or was too busy to stop. Mrs Garland, however, not wanting anyone to cast aspersions on her management skills, brooked no argument. Susan would be despatched from the department in what felt like, to her, disgrace or banishment from the sunshine of her place of honour near her heroine. She visibly slumped as she slunk away.

Glancing after her, Mrs Garland sighed and shook her head complacently.

"She's so devoted to me, poor thing," she called across the floor to Mrs Jackson.

Mrs Jackson shook her head back in return but for very different reasons. "Poor wee thing, poor little Not Now Susan," she thought.

During these breaks, fifteen minutes morning and afternoon and a whole hour for lunch, Susan paced the staff areas disconsolately. She walked aimlessly up and down the many flights of staff stairs, paused in the locker room as long as she dared and found a quiet stock room where she could eat her packed lunch. From time to time she anxiously checked her watch, counting down the time until she could return to the cosy glow of the Hosiery department.

Mrs Garland, while an obviously self-absorbed person, sure that she was absolutely correct in all her views (especially those that were completely wrong, in the opinion of others), had become aware of the young girl's regard for her. She was flattered by the enormous respect of this unexpected acolyte. She became increasingly fond of Susan and accustomed to her automatic agreement. Susan was a willing worker, always happy to do any heavy lifting or leg work that might spare Mrs Garland any effort at all. After a while, Mrs Garland began to wonder why Susan prevaricated so often when told to go for her break. She discussed it with her friend Mrs Morton from Perfumery when they were in the canteen one day.

"I can't understand why she seems to avoid breaks," she confided to Mrs Morton.

"Maybe she's fallen out with her pals in the canteen?" offered her friend.

"That's just it though. I don't think she has any pals in the canteen. I mean I've never heard her mention any and no one's ever popped in to the department to see her, you know the way they do."

The two women pondered this. Surely everyone had a group whose breaks tended to coincide and who drifted together to form vaguely age-appropriate tables? Could it be that Susan had somehow missed out on this natural Murrays development?

"I'll check with Mrs Collins. She'll know the regulars." Mrs Garland heaved herself to her feet and puffed over to the counter. Mrs Collins, having finished the cooking and preparation of the food, was perched behind the till enjoying a leisurely cigarette.

"Mrs Collins, can you tell me who my Susan is

friends with? I mean, what table does she usually join?" asked Mrs Garland.

"Susan?" queried Mrs Collins. "Young Susan. I know who you mean, I've seen her in your department, but she never comes up here. I thought she maybe went out for breaks or brought in sandwiches or something."

"What? She doesn't come up here at all?"

Mrs Collins shook her head, then turned to the person patiently waiting to pay for a steaming plateful of stovies.

Mrs Garland returned to her table, where Mrs da Costa from Accounts had now joined them. They were old friends, or at least both were long standing members of staff. Mrs Morton had filled her in on Mrs Garland's concern about her assistant. Mrs da Costa waved her hand dismissively.

"Lots of people don't come to the canteen."

Mrs Garland looked around the packed room dubiously.

"Most people do, though," she reposted.

"Take my Martin for example," Mrs da Costa continued. The other two women groaned internally. It was always a matter of time before Mrs da Costa introduced the topic of her son, now a byword for excellence in sales in the Model Gowns Department. His frankness, which was breath-taking at times, had gained the confidence and admiration of the cream of Edinburgh's society ladies. He was a most unusual young man, but much valued by the management (and his mother).

"He doesn't like the canteen at all," her voice rang out and was noted by Mrs Collins whose lips tightened.

"He says it's too noisy and smelly and the food is indigestible."

That's it, thought Mrs Collins. *I'll be serving her tiny portions from now on. Who knows, maybe even some fag ash might accidentally fall into them,* she resolved with a sniff. *Indigestible indeed!*

Unaware of the offence caused, Mrs Garland ploughed on. "But it's not natural for a young *girl* not to have friends." This was a sore point for Mrs da Costa. They had often discussed Martin's solitary nature.

"Maybe she's just shy, or an old-fashioned homebody?" offered Mrs Morton.

"I've never heard much about her family right enough." Mrs Garland frowned "Actually, I've never heard her say much about anything at all." She lapsed inwardly to search her soul. "I'll need to try harder with her, she's a good girl," she continued thoughtfully. The conversation moved on.

Over the next few days, Susan became aware of Mrs Garland watching her. She would turn around from making an adjustment to a display stand and find her boss staring. Susan wondered what she had done wrong. In another unsettling development, Mrs Garland seemed to have become noticeably nicer to her. Her mind reeled. What was going on? What could she have done wrong? She was almost glad to hear the familiar phrase "Not now, Susan," as she attempted to interject that the item a particular customer had asked for was indeed available in other shades. She withdrew gratefully until the customer moved on.

She was taken completely by surprise one Monday morning when Mrs Garland asked about her weekend. In an off-hand way, the older woman asked, "I suppose you spend most of your time with your boyfriend?"

"A boyfriend?" stammered Susan, "Oh no. I've not got a, never had a, a, a, boyfriend. Mother says…" She lapsed into awkward silence. Mrs Garland was sorry to have embarrassed the girl, but she continued, "Well, there are lots of other girls to hang around with then? I bet you have lots of fun with them."

There was a long silence. Susan looked away, "No. I don't seem to have girl friends as such. I'm just with Mum and Dad really. I like it," she said, suddenly defiant. In a rare show of discretion, Mrs Garland quietened and busied herself tidying the already immaculate sales desk.

A few days later, Mrs Garland started her enquiries again.

"So, who's the favourite pin-up of you young girls these days?" she asked casually.

Susan blushed. "I rather like Tom Selleck. You know, Magnum PI. We watch it every week. Never miss it," she admitted.

"Magnum PI," exclaimed Mrs G. "The pushy,

shouting man with the big moustache?"

"Well I don't like the moustache," Susan conceded, nodding. "But he always knows what's right and what's the best thing to do. He's sort of in charge." Her voice dwindled as she finished the sentence.

"Well I never! I couldn't abide being bossed around." Mrs Garland contemplated her husband – small and malleable and much the better for it too. She shook her head.

Over the next few months, Susan settled into a comfortable routine at work. She grew in confidence as she became more familiar with the work involved in Hosiery and even began to have her own customers: ladies who sought her out in particular. Mrs Garland noted this with mixed pleasure, but eventually, magnanimously, she admitted to Mrs Jackson that Susan's kind heart and quiet personality endeared her to some.

"She just lets them rattle on about their personal problems. I've told her not to encourage them, but, bless her, she's a kind wee soul and told me that she doesn't like to think of them going home sad. As if anything she said would make a difference," she scoffed.

But make a difference it did. Soon, almost every day, Susan was holding court, an attentive listener to one or other lady, each with a troubled expression on their face. They usually left the department with an expensive parcel of goods and a smiling countenance. Takings were up in Hosiery.

Naturally, Mrs Garland took the credit and continued in her usual domineering way. Susan remained happy to exist in orbit around her.

Despite her new-found confidence in her work and the appreciation for her empathetic manner, Susan still found breaks a trial. She avoided the canteen and wandered around the staff side of the building until it was time to return to the department. Occasionally, during her perambulations, she passed another member of staff similarly unaccompanied. She would drop her eyes to avoid looking directly at Mr da Costa as he hurried past her up the stairs or along an access corridor. Once he stopped, turned around, frowned at her and called out, "Lose the hairband," before walking purposefully on.

Susan tentatively reached up to the offending item. She eased it off, but her hair flopped forward over her face so she retied it thoughtfully. *Tonight,* she thought, *I'll try out a new style.*

The next day her arrival in the department was greeted by a gasp, "Oh Susan! What have you done to your hair?" This was called out in a complimentary manner by Mrs Garland, who continued, "It looks so much nicer. We can see your face now."

Susan ducked her head in an attempt to cover her blushes, but she was very pleased with the result of hours in front of the mirror the previous night. Indeed, compliments flew all morning as the Lingerie staff arrived and the porters delivered the latest boxes of new stock. Susan hardly knew where to look. She really only wanted to hear Mr da Costa's opinion on her new style. For once in her life she could hardly wait for lunch break.

At 12.30 Mrs Garland noticed that Susan was looking at her watch impatiently.

"Do you want to go for lunch break now?" she asked and was surprised at Susan's rapid response as she grabbed her handbag and rushed off.

Well I never, thought Mrs Garland.

After a quick visit to the Junior Staff Ladies Room to check that her hair was behaving itself, Susan tried to walk slowly up the back stairs. She hovered agitatedly for a brief moment outside the back entrance to Model Gowns, then resolutely walked up to the access corridor on the top floor of the building. Once there, she slowly paced until she heard a familiar measured step on the stairs. It was him. She turned and casually walked towards the top of the stairs. On seeing her, Mr da Costa dropped his eyes and might have walked past her, but, seeing this, she hesitatingly called out "Mr da Costa..."

He looked alarmed, but was inwardly pleased she had initiated an interaction. "Yes? Ah! I see you've done your hair as I suggested. Much better. Very much better. The hairband made you look like an overgrown schoolgirl." He scrutinised her from head to toe, "In fact you could do with shortening that skirt by one and a half inches. Where it sits now makes your calves look fat."

Susan absorbed these comments with a slight

pang before remembering that he had been right about her hair and he was famous for his relentless tactlessness. Seeing that she seemed lost for words, he swept forward.

"Come down here and I'll show you what I mean." Silently, she followed him to an old sofa stored in a corner, a relic left months ago by the porters as a job for another day.

"Sit down," he ordered. Mutely, she obeyed, glad he had taken over the situation. From his pockets he produced a small pin cushion and proceeded without explanation to pin up her hem. She leaned back against the back of the sofa and wondered what to say. He seemed happily occupied in his task. She stood up when instructed to let him finish the back. He stood back.

"That's much better," he pronounced.

"Is it?" she faltered.

"Yes," was the resounding response. "Now take it off so it can be properly sewn up; one of the seamstresses will do it right away."

She quailed "I can't. I can't just take off my skirt, not here, not now." She blushed hotly.

Giving the matter some thought, he agreed. "Well, bring it in tomorrow morning and I'll get it seen to then." Abruptly, he stood up and walked away.

In confusion, Susan called after him, "Mr da Costa?"

"Martin," he called back without turning. "Call me Martin." She smiled broadly, happy for some unknown reason.

That afternoon Martin was surprised to find himself thinking of the girl on the sixth floor as he called her. He liked her quiet, undemanding presence and the way she did as instructed without demur. With her, there was none of the inane chatter he usually experienced from his customers. He regarded this prattle as part of his job and the customers as necessary evils, although he did enjoy transforming their appearance for the better. He thought more about the girl and resolved to discuss the matter with his mother.

That evening he startled Mrs da Costa over their evening meal, usually consumed in silence, by asking her, "Do you think I should get a girlfriend?"

She choked on her cottage pie. Somehow the prospect of Martin and a girlfriend had never crossed her mind. She had been resigned to his living with them for the foreseeable future. Girlfriends led to fiancées and fiancées to wives. Martin married?

Her thoughts raced ahead.

"Well, that might be nice," she responded guardedly, "Do you have anyone in mind?"

"I met a nice quiet girl at work. That's all. I just wondered." He pointedly went on chewing and looked away, the subject at an end. Accustomed to his abrupt conversational style, Mrs da Costa continued with her meal in silence, tantalised by his response and resolving to make enquiries the next day. Surely somebody would know who this mystery girl was?

Throughout this brief conversation, her husband had remained behind his newspaper. After Martin left the table, he lowered the paper and looked at his wife questioningly.

"Well, that's a turn up, isn't it?"

"Certainly is," she responded mildly. Her world had just tilted on its axis. "Do you think John, oh do you think, maybe it's a sign that he's…" The word 'normal' hovered unspoken between them.

"He's just not usually a people person," he replied severely. "He's not one for frivolous friends."

"Or any friends really," she added knowingly. She and her husband had frequently discussed Asperger syndrome in connection with their boy.

"Indeed," was the response as the paper was raised once more, indicating that the discussion was at an end. Mrs da Costa retreated into her own thoughts. With a sigh, she contemplated that once far distant, but now just possible, Holy Grail for ladies of a certain age: grandchildren.

Across town a similar meal was taking place. No one was reading of course, but Susan's parents' polite silences were always alert for the requirement to pass something to one or other of the family. They were a very courteous family, anxious to be as helpful as possible. Good listeners are not often prolific talkers and the Harrisons were extremely good listeners. After Susan left the table intent on hemming her skirt, Mrs Harrison looked at her husband. "Susan's looking very…" she hesitated, uncertain of how to describe Susan's discernible glow.

"Yes," replied her husband in agreement. The subject was then, for the Harrisons, closed.

Slowly, very slowly, over the next few weeks and months, Martin and Susan began to see more of each other. It became accepted between them that they would meet at lunch break on the abandoned sofa on the top corridor. Unspoken, this arrangement was sometimes broken by one or other due to departmental expediency or the vagaries of demanding customers. When this happened the one left sitting by him or herself felt unaccountably bereft. Susan would be sorry to miss out on hearing about the latest outrage in Model Gowns or the ups and downs of the fortunes of certain football teams. She seldom contributed much herself other than encouraging nods and indications of interest. For his part, Martin found himself preparing topics of interest (to him) the night before. It never crossed his mind that she wouldn't be as fascinated as he was by goal averages and other football statistics. He appreciated her clear explanations of what customers might have meant when they said certain things or why they had reacted to something he said. He began to understand what people meant by empathy. More than that though, he began to dwell on her clear blue eyes and soft complexion. He thought about the inviting curves beneath her uniform in a way that he had never thought of them on his customers. He began to have unsettling dreams. He missed her undemanding presence when she wasn't there. He really missed her...

Susan now spent a great deal of time on her personal appearance, prompted by Martin's caustic comments on any transgression of style. She knew this was not personal in any way; it was merely constructive criticism on his part. He was, after all, famous for turning out society ladies at their absolute best. As she restyled her hair or thought up different combinations of skirts and blouses, she sometimes let her thoughts wander further than just shared lunch breaks. She was proud to have such a handsome boyfriend and felt safe with him in charge. She began to long for closer proximity on the sofa. Once, he had impulsively taken her hand and she went over this exciting memory each night, wondering how she could create a situation where he did so again. Or more.

Feeling so much smarter, Susan's confidence improved greatly and Mrs Garland wondered what was going on. Her question was answered one lunchtime when a small, insignificant lady of indeterminate age walked hesitatingly into the department. She approached the counter. "Mrs Garland?" she asked politely.

"Yes Madam. Can I help you?" Mrs Garland replied cautiously. This didn't look like a typical customer.

"I wonder if you can? I'm Susan's mother."

Mrs Garland nodded and Mrs Harrison

continued, "We were wondering if, by any chance, you knew who this Martin might be?"

"Martin?"

"Yes, Susan's been talking about a Martin such a lot at home and it's not like her, not like her at all and she looks so different too…" she lapsed, looking hopefully at Mrs Garland.

"Sit down Mrs Harrison," Mrs Garland indicated the little chair drawn up at the counter. "I think I might know who you mean."

The news was out. The canteen smirked at the thought of Not Now Susan and Mr da Costa the scathing wonder salesman from Model Gowns.

"Fancy Susan and that Mr da Costa getting together," laughed Shirley from China and Glass, who had long harboured intentions towards him. Asperger syndrome or not, he was a fine-looking young man.

"He'll boss her around no end," put in Audrey. "I wouldn't put up with any man pushing me around."

"Of course some girls like that sort of thing, if they're a bit shy or something," mused Shirley.

"Wimps!" was the scornful response, "Not exactly feminist."

"Not everyone is," said Irene the Florist, defensively. She liked Susan. "There's plenty of old-fashioned girls around. Susan must be one of them."

"Well, good luck to her is all I can say," added Audrey. They all nodded, then moved on to discussing the royal wedding.

One grey February day up in the top floor corridor, sandwiches safely consumed, Martin stood up to indicate that lunch break was over. Susan scrambled to her feet too and to her surprise, he suddenly turned towards her.

"Right," he barked, "I'll get the ring, shall I?"

"Erm if you want to Martin," she replied cautiously, uncertain what he meant.

"Well I'll have to."

"Will you?"

"Of course. If we're going to get married, we'll need to be engaged first."

"Married?"

"Yes. We've been together for a year now. That's what usually happens. I've been reading about it."

"Have you," she replied faintly.

"Yes."

She turned towards him. He looked down into her eyes. Her clear, blue eyes. She looked up trustingly.

"Martin?" she queried.

"Not now, Susan," he said as he leaned in to kiss her.

The old-fashioned girl glowed with happiness.

Chapter 9

Pegram's Progress

Louise Pegram (née Jones) was easily the most popular person working at Murrays. Nobody had a bad word to say about her (except Mr McElvey in his periodic rants against extravagance). She had a listening ear for everyone and her door was, quite literally, always open. Her kindness, tact and sympathy extended to everyone from the newest recruit to the oldest retired member of staff. She kept in touch with the Murrays' pensioners and organised a Christmas get together for them each year. She attended staff weddings, their children's christenings and, from time to time, funerals. There was, it would seem, no end to her keen involvement with every aspect of her work and the people that it comprised.

It was not as if she'd had a happy, settled life herself. She was able to be so understanding because she had been dealt a severe blow by life and had suffered deeply due to this. She knew emotional pain well. Her husband of only two years had been killed on active duty in the army in Northern Ireland. An IRA bomb had ripped her life apart as surely as it had murdered him. Their marriage was in its earliest, happiest stage when it was so cruelly severed. At first she didn't understand how she could possibly go on. In the depths of her misery she had contemplated ending it all, but shied away from this as she pondered what her Iain would have said. So she picked herself up and reviewed her options.

Louise was a trained social worker. This had been useful in the army. As an officer's wife she was expected to be involved in the welfare of the men and their families. She was adept at the paperwork involved and had completed further training to keep her up to date with the relevant legislation. Thus, she was well equipped to take up Margaret Murray's offer of employment as a Personnel Officer in the first dark days of her widowhood. Margaret was a long-time friend from their tennis-playing youth. The job offer was a godsend in more ways than one; she needed distraction, but also, immediately after Iain's death her financial situation was not good. The various pensions and insurance policies were slowly making their way through to his estate, but not at the pace she required. She needed a job and the salary that came with it.

In time, her skills in personnel led to her being promoted to Personnel Manager and she gained a place on the management board. The various eventual financial settlements enabled her to buy a small house in a quiet suburb and her life was set into a pattern. In actual fact, the army widows' pension was such that she didn't need to work but, by then, she couldn't contemplate what she would do without the all-enveloping nature of her involvement with Murrays department store.

Her little house became her sanctuary and she scuttled home thankfully at the end of each demanding day. Her elderly neighbour, Evie, would watch out for her return with some satisfaction. She had befriended Louise from the day she moved in and became a reliable source of local information, gossip and scones. Evie held the spare set of keys to Louise's house and, although technically this was only to receive parcels or admit tradesmen as required, she looked after the house too. Louise would return each evening to a freshly tidied house, the washing done and clean sheets on the bed. Sometimes a casserole would be simmering in the oven too. She had remonstrated with Evie often enough over the years, but Evie laughed off Louise's protests saying she enjoyed having someone to look after. The two women became firm friends across the generational divide. Some evenings, over a glass of sherry, they would discuss Louise's day; Evie had sound counsel to offer regarding the various problems Louise faced with Murrays' staff members. She often had advice for Louise herself too. She worried about Louise's almost total immersion in her work. She was always encouraging her to get out and about more and to meet people outside the intense little world of Murrays.

One bright Sunday morning, Louise woke early, cursing her inability to sleep in. She went downstairs to the kitchen and made herself a cup of tea. Taking it outside to the sunny patio, she settled on a bench and, closing her eyes, turned her face towards the sun, revelling in the unexpected early morning warmth. She had meant to bring out her book to read but had left it on her bedside table. Overcome with inertia, she stretched and leant back in her seat. Her mind wandered randomly as she considered her life, but suddenly it crystallised into one striking thought: Is this it? Is this what my life consists of? Is there nothing else for me? She supposed these were the classic midlife considerations, but they nagged insistently at her. She was always encouraging others to think about how they could move on in their lives, to make the most of themselves. Why shouldn't this encouragement apply to herself? Why not indeed.

Now sitting bolt upright with her eyes open, blinking against the sunlight, she went over and over this question. After a while, shaking her head as though to dislodge the thought, she got up and returned to the kitchen. The sun had, metaphorically, gone in. Busying herself with household chores, she was able to bury the uncomfortable thought for the rest of the day, but she was left with an awareness that something was wrong in her world.

The next evening, on her return from work, she found Evie had been in again. The day's mail was propped up on a mug next to a plate of tiny cakes on her kitchen table. One of the letters carried an American stamp. Recognising the postmark, Louise smiled and pocketed the letter, looking forward to reading it later at leisure. She went into the kitchen to start to make her supper.

Later, all household tasks done, she sat in her sitting room, glass of sherry to hand, as she put on her new reading glasses and opened the letter. It was from her old friend Helen. Helen was another ex-army wife. The two had become close friends in adversity when Helen's husband was also killed in action. The two women had stayed in touch over the years and Louise enjoyed hearing of Helen's exploits. Unlike Louise, Helen had not wanted to settle down. She was slightly older than Louise and had experienced more of the constant moves required of army families. She had become accustomed to the peripatetic style of life and, after her husband's death, had continued in this fashion. Eventually, she had settled in a small town in Virginia USA and had found happiness in a new husband and job there. Her updates on small town life kept Louise amused and she often thought she should visit her friend. As her eyes moved over the letter, it seemed this day might have come.

Instead of the usual descriptions of neighbours' barbecues or the purchase of snow tyres, the letter earnestly invited her to visit, indeed to make a permanent visit. It seemed that the local area was crying out for experienced social workers. Housing and transport was available, as was a good salary. Newington Virginia needed her. Helen assured her that she would do everything she could to introduce Louise to all her friends and neighbours and to make her life as much fun as possible. She even hinted about the availability of a preponderance of handsome, unattached men. Her eyes widening, Louise took a deep inward breath and continued to the end of the letter. It ended with a reiteration of the offer, begging her to consider it seriously. A newspaper cutting was enclosed concerning the town's dire need of good social workers.

She sat back and lost herself in the contemplation of this offer. Was this the answer to yesterday's query? Strange how life throws up these things. What should she do? What could she do? Her sensible mind responded with a series of options: she could just do it, she could refuse, she could visit just to see, she could, she could, she could...There were so many reasons to take up the offer and so many to refuse it.

Louise felt confused and unsettled as her internal debate raged that night and on into the next few days. She wished she had someone to discuss it with. She hesitated to confide in Margaret who would definitely want her to remain at Murrays.

Louise had a vague, worrying feeling about Murrays beginning to lose its place in the hearts and minds of local shoppers. Nothing explicit, just a very slight downward turn in the accounts. Margaret might need her support.

Evie would be devastated if she moved away. She knew how important she was to her two dear friends. As ever, she asked herself what Iain would have done. She felt bereft all over again.

Evie, as though sensing something was up, appeared the next evening, letting herself in through the back door. Louise was always pleased to see her and offered her a cup of tea. The two settled down for a chat. Louise considered taking the bull by the horns and bringing up the subject of Virginia, but Evie cut in before she could start.

"Now dear, I've been thinking about you. You're obviously not happy. I've said it before and I'll say it again, you need some outside interests." Louise tried to speak, but Evie ploughed on regardless, "There's a nice ladies group I've found out about. It's for professional women like yourself. They meet each week in a room at the Anchor Hotel and they have speakers and suchlike and go on outings and things like that. You might make some nice new friends," she finished hopefully.

"Oh Evie, it's not my sort of thing," Louise started, but was interrupted.

"I won't be here forever you know, you'll need some local friends and contacts." It was an old argument and one that Louise knew she could never win. With bad grace, she agreed to go along to the next meeting and at least see what it was like. Evie nodded with satisfaction.

The following Tuesday, Louise walked uncertainly into the Anchor Hotel. A typewritten note affixed to the door told her that the ladies group was in the back room immediately to the left of the bar. She entered the room quietly and found a seat for herself in the back row. Others smiled in greeting and two of the ladies came up to her to introduce themselves and welcome her. They encouraged her to sit with them and introduced everyone as they entered. They seemed a friendly crowd. The speaker that evening was a local baker and she enjoyed hearing his stories of the renovation of the old bake house. Afterwards, many of the assembled ladies went through to the bar for a glass of wine. Joining them at their request, Louise found herself thoroughly enjoying the mental distraction of it all and was glad she had come. She decided to formally join the group and paid her small subscription fee. She was given a newsletter outlining all the forthcoming talks and events. She told herself that, even if she did decide to go to Virginia, the small subscription fee was so negligible that it could be looked on as a donation.

The following week the talk was by a floral artist, and the next was a minister talking about a trip to a war-torn country. Louise was slightly surprised therefore, on entering the meeting room a fortnight later, to discover that the planned speaker had cancelled and a last-minute speaker had been substituted. A small, nondescript lady was shown in and took a seat at the front, facing the assembled ladies. The secretary introduced her as Mrs Evans and assumed everyone knew her. Most of the group did seem to know her and several leaned forward expectantly. Louise sat back, not knowing what to expect, but not really caring either. It had been another busy day at work and all she wanted was a diversion.

Mrs Evans looked humbly at the group and started by saying that she couldn't guarantee anything but she would do her best. Puzzled, Louise looked on. The woman on her left nudged her and whispered, "I've heard she's really good."

At this point Mrs Evans, with eyes tight shut, suddenly sat bolt upright. "Atten...shun!" she said. Her voice changed slightly, it deepened and she continued in almost a caressing tone, "Oh Dafty, Dafty, don't do it. Be where you're needed. Think big. Think far away." Her voice faded.

In her seat, Louise felt icy cold all over. Iain had always called her Dafty. It was his pet name for her. He called her Dafty because she was so clever. No one else knew that. Surely nobody else was ever called that as an endearment. Her mind reeled. She felt momentarily sick. The woman in front turned in her seat and looked at her sympathetically, "Was that for you? You're so lucky. I've been hoping for a message from my Gran for years. I always go along to Mrs Evan's meetings."

Louise stared into space for the rest of the session. By the time Mrs Evans left, several women were in tears of happiness and one sat, white faced, apparently unable to move. Everyone else clapped and the secretary rose to thank her. It had been a very good evening for Mrs Evans.

Louise didn't join her new friends for a drink that evening; instead she hurried home. She wanted to be alone with her thoughts. What did it all mean? What could it possibly mean? She had never had any opinion about spiritualist mediums. She'd never even thought about them at all or, at the very least, thought that if people found comfort from them, then why not?

Iain though. Her Iain. That had felt like a very direct message especially for her. She racked her brains for an explanation, but could not think of one. The message itself intrigued her. What exactly did it mean? "Be where you're needed" sounded like she should stay where she was, but "think big, think far away," sounded like he was encouraging a move to Virginia. It was all so confusing. She tossed and turned all night but sleep eluded her.

The next morning at the management team meeting, Margaret looked at her askance,

"A bad night?" she enquired.

"Something like that."

The meeting moved on. Mr McElvey had the latest set of figures and Mr Soames had cross referenced them with the footfall. Both were indiscernibly down, but down nevertheless. Margaret was worried. Murrays was her baby and anything that affected Murrays affected her personally.

The team settled back, anticipating a long meeting that day. However, they were interrupted by Mrs Carr.

"There's a telephone call for you, Mrs Pegram. Please could you come. It sounds important." Louise got to her feet.

Back in her office Mrs Carr put the call through. It was Evie.

"Could you come home please? I'm sorry, I'm so

sorry."

Louise was immediately alert to a change in Evie's voice. Something was badly wrong at home. Grabbing her jacket and bag, she threw caution to the wind, rushing towards the front of the shop so she could hail a taxi. She was sure Mrs Carr would explain what had happened to the other managers. As she dashed out through Cosmetics and Perfumery the staff looked at each other in surprise. It wasn't like the calm, collected Mrs Pegram to look so rattled. They shrugged their shoulders and continued their work.

Back home, Louise found Evie's keys and let herself into her old neighbour's house. Evie was slumped in her chair in the sitting room looking helpless. Her face was slightly crumpled to one side and her left arm hung limply. It was clear that she'd had a stroke. Her speech was slightly slurred but comprehensible. She tried to smile at Louise but it was a sinister shadow of her usual greeting. Louise swung into action.

Fortuitously, the doctor confirmed that, although it was a stroke, it seemed to be a mild one and, indeed, Evie was recovering very quickly. He warned that it should be regarded as a warning signal and she should take it easy. The old Evie would have laughed this off, but the confidence seemed to have drained from her and she was tired and withdrawn. With Louise's contacts it was no problem organising visiting support for her old friend and life gradually resumed its old pattern, but with the balance of care changing: now it was Louise's turn to look after Evie.

And still Louise continued to ponder Iain's message. "Be where you're needed," now seemed to indicate both here with Evie and in Virginia where social workers were so desperately required. "Think big. Think far away," also indicated a move overseas, but how could she leave her old friend?

There was an additional issue. On reading the minutes of the meeting she'd left, she found to her concern and surprise that there were worrying issues facing Murrays. Change was in the air in the world of retail. The march of the chain stores appeared to be inexorable and, although not yet impinging on Murrays, Mr McElvey was urging the management team to be aware of potential trouble ahead. Louise's thoughts flew to Margaret. How worried she must be. Poor thing. She needed her too. Maybe there would be time to discuss things on their forthcoming holiday. She hoped so.

"Think big. Think far away..." Could that possibly be an allusion to their next trip?

Chapter 10

Rest and Relaxation

The management meeting was drawing to a close. Some of the usual vexed issues around succession planning and recruitment had arisen and, once again, had been deferred to the next meeting. Miss Murray collated her papers and looked up,

"Gentleman, just to remind you that Louise and I will be off on our annual holiday for two weeks. We're leaving on Saturday and won't be back until the 14th of June. I trust you'll be able to hold things together until then?" she asked challengingly. "No fighting boys!" she continued with a laugh.

Mr McElvey drew himself up stiffly, "I think you know you can count on us."

Mr Philipson and Mr Soames exchanged glances. Miss Murray's annual holiday was an ideal chance for Mr McElvey to rush through edicts which would not otherwise be passed. They well remembered the debacle last year when he instituted a system of staff fines for minor transgressions. Mrs Pegram had returned to a huge queue of disgruntled employees, much to the delight of Jim Hudson, the Union Rep. It had taken weeks to sort out and in the meantime the fining system was quietly dropped.

Miss Murray did worry about leaving her precious store but was aware that she had to go away for at least two weeks. This was not on her own account, but to allow the Glens and the Joshis time for a break. The Glens tended to go "doon the watter" when Miss Murray was away. Indeed, Mrs Glen had once memorably informed her quite earnestly that, "We do like to be beside the seaside."

The Joshis had recently made contact with a distant cousin whose family were now located in Birmingham and they planned to visit. It had been years since they had seen the family. Mrs Joshi was particularly excited about the trip and the lodge house at Rosehill was a flurry of packing and baking special sweets to take with them.

Mrs Pegram and Miss Murray had not always holidayed together. For years Miss Murray would take herself off to one or other of the large resort hotels where she tried to blend in with the many large families enjoying the organised activities. However, her solitary state was heavily emphasised at meal times as she took her seat at a table for one. Staff were always particularly kind and tried extra hard to do their best for her, but somehow that made it worse. Eventually, she had confided this to Louise, who completely agreed with her. She generally went on holiday with her brother and his boisterous family. However, she always felt like a spare wheel or worse when her sister-in-law made her annual clumsy attempt to introduce her to an unattached male friend. The two women decided then and there to holiday together.

Some years they went abroad, often to the South of France or the Italian Riviera, but they got fed up with all the travel required. As Miss Murray put it,

"It's quite exciting on the way out, but the trip back with all our luggage to carry through the stations and the interminable railway journeys are just awful. I always arrive back tired out."

"We could try flying?" Louise suggested when they were making plans one year, but Miss Murray wasn't keen. She was surprisingly cautious, Louise thought. "What about a cruise?" she put forward.

"Maybe" Miss Murray replied noncommittally. "I'll have a think about it."

Naturally, by the time she made up her mind to go on a cruise around the historical sights of Greece, it was all booked up. Discussing this disappointment over coffee one morning, Louise hesitantly mentioned another idea. "Would you consider a very different sort of holiday?" she wondered. "More of a change than a rest."

"Go on," said Miss Murray, intrigued.

"Well I was wondering about the Outer Hebrides. Maybe a small island? We'd not have to do anything but read, walk, maybe do some bird watching or something? I'd like some thinking time. Just a bit of time out of ordinary life. I hear it's like stepping back decades on some of the islands."

"You've got this all planned out, haven't you?" laughed Miss Murray.

"Well I have done a bit of research," her friend admitted. Seeing Miss Murray's interest, she continued, "I'd thought of Shepsay. It's only small but it's reachable by ferry and there's a Bed and Breakfast where we could stay," she added hopefully.

The ferry crossing on the MS Clonaghty was uneventful from a motion point of view. The sea was like glass. Margaret, as Louise felt able to call her when on their own, had worried about a recurrence of her girlhood tendency to 'mal de mer,' but all went well.

There were several slight contretemps, however, with a rather pushy young man who elbowed past rudely at the rails as they drew away from Oban; he wanted to take a last photograph. Margaret and Louise exchanged looks with raised eyebrows and Margaret whispered, "American!"

Louise responded, "Typical!" They turned away from the side of the ship, shivering slightly in the sea breeze and, opening the heavy door, entered the lounge. They sat for a moment looking around, then Louise said, "How about a drink? The bar windows have better views."

"Good idea. Soft drinks only for you though," Margaret said reprovingly as they stood up and moved towards the door of the ship's bar.

"I know," laughed Louise, pushing the door open. They scanned the crowded room looking for a seat. There was space for two on a bench seat under a window. They moved towards it, threading their way between the crowded tables. When they reached it, Margaret turned politely to Louise to indicate that she should sit first, but at that exact point the American slipped deftly into the seat and placed his photographic gear on the remaining space. The two ladies looked at him askance.

"Excuse me young man but we were just on the point of sitting here," burst out Margaret.

"You snooze you lose," he replied unconcernedly rifling through his camera bag. Finding the booklet he was searching for he looked up. "Hope you find somewhere to sit though. You look like you could do with a rest." Appalled at his rudeness, the ladies gasped. Margaret opened her mouth to tell him what she thought of that particular comment but, to Louise's relief, thought better of it. Other passengers were beginning to stare and so the ladies retreated to the lounge.

"Well, really." Louise exclaimed. The barman, who saw what happened, came to see if he could bring them a drink in the lounge.

"No thanks. I just don't feel like anything now," said Margaret gloomily. Not a great start to the holiday, she thought.

Louise nosed the Austin cautiously out of the ferry's hold and down the steep ramp. Ahead of them, a trickle of cars disappeared up a narrow road and veered off to the left behind a low hill. A rather seedy-looking pub crouched immediately to their right as they left the short pier. Already the ferrymen could be seen running in for a quick drink before setting off back to Oban.

On either side of the road an assortment of cottages and other smallish buildings were spread out in a haphazard manner. As the car progressed slowly along, they noticed a garage, a doctor's surgery and a newsagent. On a hillside further up the road a church and its attendant manse looked down on the little township. There were few people about; just some children who watched the ferry's arrival and disgorging of passengers and cars with listless interest. It was clear that Shepsay lacked something in the way of entertainment.

Louise drove up the hill. The road followed the rocky contours of the rugged island. They were booked to stay with a Mrs McNeil at Farbost. She had been assured that if they followed the road around the island, they couldn't fail to spot her house: it was white. Margaret eagerly looked about her as they drove slowly on. The road was narrow with just a few passing places and Louise, who was a nervous driver and dreaded meeting a car coming in the opposite direction, watched the road closely. They passed several small crofts, each time urged on their way by suicidal collies who rushed straight at the car barking wildly and chasing them down the road. Every house was painted white.

Eventually, after what seemed like many miles, but was perhaps only ten, they saw a little sign by the roadside announcing that they had arrived at their destination. "Farbost, Bed and Breakfast and Emporium". "Hot and Cold available" was added as a further inducement to any potentially reluctant customer. Margaret frowned. "Oh Louise. Where have you brought us?"

Smiling brightly, Louise responded, "A change is as good as a rest and look, they have hot and cold," she pointed out.

"Hot and cold what though," Margaret responded, but couldn't continue as a little woman had emerged from the house and was knocking on the car window.

"Are you the ladies from the city?" she enquired in a strong west Highland accent. She introduced herself as Mrs McNeil. "Welcome, welcome. Come away in and we'll have a wee cup of tea."

Over tea in the low ceilinged, immaculately clean and fully knick-knacked sitting room, Mrs McNeil outlined the rules and regulations for their stay. Breakfast was at 8am sharp. A sandwich lunch would be provided and the evening meal would be at 5.30pm. A late supper would be brought through to them at 10pm. She trusted that would be acceptable. It was. The ladies departed for their bedrooms. On the inspection of which, each was uneasily aware that, judging by the overflowing drawers and bulging wardrobes, the family had been recently evicted to make way for their guests.

After unpacking (as much as possible), the two ladies went out for a walk. They found themselves accompanied by a silent and dejected collie. He cringed from their attempts to pat him but followed determinedly as they walked across the machair to the beach. It stretched out on either side in a pearly white strand, leading on to an almost unnaturally blue sea. Gulls wheeled overhead. The fresh breeze from the sea made conversation difficult, but neither wanted to speak, just to absorb the natural beauty of the place. Looking back at the cottage, they could see that an awkward extension was attached to one side. It looked temporary and had a sway-backed roof, but was nevertheless connected to the cottage by overhead wires for the electricity and a telephone line.

"That must be the Emporium," Louise said, stating the obvious. They set off back to the cottage, the depressed dog at their heels.

The next few days passed in the peaceful, rather passive enjoyment of doing nothing in particular. This was a real treat for the two ladies who were usually so busy. They lapsed into a gentle routine of gigantic breakfasts, huge picnic lunches and colossal evening meals with a final mammoth snack before they staggered, replete, to bed and slept like logs. They were stunned by the sheer quantity of food they consumed. They walked in the fresh air, watched birds, took photographs and tried to sketch some of the old buildings they found scattered around the island. Little by little they succumbed to island time: measured by meals, Sundays and the ferry timetable.

One fresh morning, returning from a pre-breakfast stroll down to the beach, they were met by the sight of an agitated Mrs McNeil in her best coat peering anxiously at them. She was holding a small suitcase. Clearly there was some sort of problem. Breaking into a trot, Louise got there first. "What's up Mrs McNeil?" she asked.

"It's my daughter, Dolina, in Glasgow. The baby's come early. I'll have to get down there to help out with the other children. I'm afraid you'll have to go. If you pack quickly we can catch the ten o'clock ferry."

Her thoughts racing for what felt like the first time in days, Margaret rapidly assessed the situation. "No, you go, we can fend for ourselves. You can trust us." She looked reassuringly at the little woman.

"I do, I do, it's not that. It's not just the house. It's the shop too," she sighed.

Margaret and Louise exchanged glances. Louise nodded as Margaret continued, "We'll run the shop if that would help," she offered bravely. The three women looked at each other. "We've experience in that sort of thing," Louise cut in. Mrs McNeil, by now desperate to get away, thrust a set of keys into their hands and set off for the bus stop where the little bus had been waiting for her, the driver alerted to her predicament by the island bush telegraph.

After a scratch breakfast, the two ladies went out to inspect the 'Emporium,' their temporary new empire.

The shed in which it was housed was chilly and the atmosphere slightly damp. The light from the single bulb dangling dangerously from the ceiling cast a feeble glow over the disparate range of products. There appeared to be no particular logic to the display and tins of beans were interspersed with boxes of Elastoplast and teabags. Everything in the shed was rather dusty with tatty packaging and out of date labels.

Margaret and Louise exchanged glances.

"This will never do," said Margaret. "We can do Mrs McNeil a big favour by sorting all this out and organising the shop into a more efficient display and layout." She eyed the ancient till and prodded its keys. "We've no float either. I just hope the customers will have change, or maybe there's still some in the damned thing but I can't work out how to open it." She frowned.

Meanwhile Louise disappeared into the house, re-emerging some minutes later with a bucket of hot water and a sponge.

Margaret tussled with the recalcitrant till and then joined Louise who had set to trying to clean and impose some logical order on the shelves. The two worked with a will; by 11am they felt ready to face any customers and Louise threw open the door. The depressed collie standing guard outside looked at them and sighed. No one else was in sight. After a while Margaret went to make a cup of tea as Louise sat behind the makeshift counter. On Margaret's return she looked enquiringly at her, "Anything doing?"

Louise shook her head. "We've been open for ages now and not a single customer."

Margaret grimaced. Suddenly the dog sneezed, startling them. They looked up at this and saw a lone figure, well wrapped up, making his or her way down the path to the shop. The ladies sprang to attention as s/he entered. "Good morning," they chorused brightly and rather too hopefully.

"You'll be the ladies playing at shops?" the lone figure, now revealed as a tiny elderly man, stated, ignoring their greeting.

"Well I don't know about playing," said Margaret defensively, "We're holding the fort for Mrs McNeil if that's what you mean."

"What can we help you with today?" cut in Louise smoothly.

"Nothing," came the reply. "The Co-operative van will be here soon." With that he turned and walked off back up the path, leaving the ladies dumbfounded at his rudeness. He wasn't the last to visit though. Over the course of the long day there was an irregular trickle of customers each on some feeble pretext, but plainly just there to have a look at the 'ladies playing at shops'. The friendliest of them went so far as to speak directly to Margaret.

"What have you done to Christina's good shop? Ah canna find onything." She looked accusingly at them.

"Well, what was it you were wanting?" asked Louise. "Maybe I can help?"

"How do I know what I want until I see it?" came the logical response, "and I canna see it," she finished triumphantly, staring at them through narrowed eyes.

Louise rose to the occasion, forestalling Margaret's likely exasperated response, "Well, do please feel free to have a lovely browse through everything."

"A browse is it? A browse? Well I never did." With that the woman walked out shaking her head and muttering to herself about never thinking she'd see the day, and her in Christina McNeil's good shop too.

Margaret and Louise looked at each other in dismay. "This is pointless." Margaret burst out. "We've been here all day, given the place a good tidy up and sort out and not sold a single thing. I think we should just shut up shop for the day." Louise agreed. Locking up the front door and switching off the light, they left by the back door directly into the house, the dejected dog at their heels mirroring how they felt. Perhaps things would be better the next day.

It wasn't. The rain beat down on the tin roof and the two women peered out hopefully through the rain streaked window. Margaret brought out her book. Louise made even more tea. Still no customers. The dog, now thoroughly bedraggled, refused to leave his post outside the door.

Suddenly, there was a flurry of activity outside. The dog barked loudly and a family in brightly coloured raincoats burst in, anxious to get out of the rain and avoid the dog.

"Blimey what have we here!" exclaimed the man looking around him.

"Who cares? It's a shop," replied his wife. The three small children scurried around turning over packets of biscuits and crisps, eagerly reaching for sweets and chocolates. Margaret struggled to keep an eye on them all. The mother engaged Louise's attention as she went through a long list of items, none of which they seemed to stock. As she finally came to the end, each item leading to a sorrowful shake of Louise's head, she burst out exasperatedly, "What no garlic? No couscous? Where am I? The end of the world? For God's sake! This is the most useless shop in the most useless place I've ever been! This is the last time I let you choose where we go on holiday."

The last comment was fired at her husband who was apologetically rounding up their unruly children.

The husband thrust a £1 note into Margaret's hand for the sweets the children had grabbed and started to consume. It didn't cover the amount, but they were glad to see the back of such unhappy customers.

Just as they were recovering from the confusion, the door was flung open and a dishevelled figure shot into the shop, slamming the door behind him. "Damn that doggone dog," he exclaimed, ruefully looking behind him. "He bit me! He got me on the wrist." He thrust his wrist towards the ladies now safely behind the counter. A red semicircle bore testimony to this.

"Oh dear. I'm so sorry," Louise began, "It's not like him." She considered, "Well I don't really know. He's not our dog."

"Well you should get rid of him," was the

snapped response, "No wonder you're struggling for customers." He looked scornfully around the shop at its sad, depleted shelves. "Some shop!"

"We do our best," replied Louise with dignity. "Now perhaps we could clean up your wrist for you?"

He grudgingly agreed to have his wrist dabbed with a clean cloth fetched from the kitchen and Margaret found a bottle of TCP which they applied generously, to the man's wincing discomfort.

"We've met before I think?" enquired Margaret in a voice Louise instantly recognised as dangerous.

"I don't think so," came the reply.

"Were you not on the boat the other week? I'm sure we saw you in the bar." Louise glared pointedly as Margaret continued. "I do hope you found it comfortable in that window seat."

He nodded, "Oh yeah, the two old dears from the bar. I probably did you a favour keeping you off the gin. Am I right or am I right?" He looked at them enquiringly. He seemed to have recovered from his injury and was on the point of laughter. There was a stunned silence. No one had ever said anything like that to either of them.

Louise recovered first, albeit stiffly. "What can we get you? Was it groceries or something else perhaps? We have a small selection of postcards if you're interested."

He looked around the shop and then, to their acute discomfiture, burst out laughing. "Jeez, I've not seen anything like this since I was a kid in

Arkansas. It's sooooo old fashioned and the stock is just awful. Thanks ladies but no thanks. Time for you to give this up. Face it girls you're obviously not cut out for retail in this century."

He made to leave, but turned at the door, "Just a minute though, think I'll take a snap. Must preserve this museum for posterity." Quickly, he took out his camera and, with a bright flash, captured the shabby little shop and its startled staff in a washed-out image that he'd pass around his friends for a glimpse of old time 'Scaaaatland'. He left. The ladies were pleased to watch his rapid retreat along the path with the dog in hot pursuit.

There was a short silence. "That dog's good for something at last," Margaret pronounced, but Louise ruefully pointed out that it could have meant trouble for Mrs McNeil if he decided to sue. However, all was well, if not necessarily prosperous.

Mrs McNeil arrived back at the end of the week with Dolina, the new baby and an assortment of younger McNeils. It was clear their rooms would be required, but by this time the ladies felt they had been on Shepsay for weeks if not months. Their days had lapsed into a relaxed routine: manning the shop, reading, serving the occasional customer and cashing up the meagre takings while meticulously recording it in the ledger they found under the counter. Mrs McNeil was thrilled that they had somehow doubled takings and thanked them from the bottom of her heart for looking after the shop. The whole family waved the ladies off on their way back to the harbour.

They discussed their stint behind a counter in the car. "If that's doubling takings, it's surely not worth her while keeping the shop open at all?" queried Margaret with her usual eye to the bottom line.

"Maybe not. Maybe it's a way of life more than anything else?" suggested Louise. Margaret nodded, "Yes. That'll be it. I bet her parents had that shop before her."

"Like you, you mean?" They both laughed.

Returning to work the next week, Louise's mind raced over what she should be doing. Her holiday had not allowed her the time she'd expected to ponder the dilemma of Iain's pronouncements. Meanwhile, Margaret mentally drew up an agenda for that day's management meeting. There was a lot to catch up on.

"And so," Mr McElvey droned on in the conclusion of a forty-minute lecture on what they had missed, "We have had a *relatively* good fortnight, although sales in the Food Hall were down."

"Thank you, Mr McElvey" Margaret nodded graciously. "Sounds like you all did very well. Now, to return to the matter we were discussing at our last meeting, have you any thoughts about recruiting new people at management level? As I said before, we're none of us getting any younger. We need some new blood. And some new ideas to help us keep up with the times."

After some discussion it was decided to advertise nationally and to wait and see what the response was before taking any firm decisions. Louise set off back to her office to draw up a job description. Margaret wanted to check it over when it was done to see if it captured exactly the sort of person they were looking for. Mr McElvey, naturally, wanted to think through the cost implications.

The next month the management team met to examine the applications for the new junior management jobs. There were some from staff at other local department stores. Several of these were earmarked to be invited for interviews. Louise was particularly pleased to find some internal applications including 'Flash' Harry Ferguson, Samantha Cooper and, surprisingly, Anjali Joshi. It was decided that each of these deserved to be taken seriously and appointments were made for their interviews. Margaret flicked through the remainder of the application forms, discarding each for different reasons, too old, too young, too frivolous and so on. She paused at one.

"Hold on, looks like a promising one here," she informed the others, "Lots of experience already, knows the market, accountancy qualifications, trained in New York. He sounds terrific, we'll need to see him."

The others nodded enthusiastically, although Mr

McElvey muttered suspiciously about some people being too good to be true.

By 4pm the following Thursday the two ladies had interviewed seven prospective new junior managers. Over a cup of tea in the boardroom they debated whether it would look bad if they favoured the internal candidates, but Harry, Samantha and Anjali had all been very impressive and had each talked with enthusiasm of different aspects of the job. Together, they had the potential to be a very effective team in a few years' time. Just what they were looking for.

Margaret was pleased about Anjali's application. Remembering the fracas and her eventual employment at Murrays, she was very glad the girl was doing so well and felt settled enough to apply to the management training scheme. Her faith in Anjali had evidently paid off. She hoped her parents were pleased with how it had all turned out.

There was only one applicant left to interview. He was due at 4.15pm. There was a knock at the door, Mrs Carr stuck her head in to say that their last interviewee had arrived. "Thank you. Show him in please," called out Louise.

They sat back expectantly, smiling warmly to put the newcomer at his ease. The smiles disappeared rapidly, however, as the new entrant sat down and confidently scanned their faces over the boardroom table.

He half stood up again and reached a hand

forward, "Hi, I'm Gary Halverson, glad to meet you and you'll be?" he enquired of Margaret who had stood up.

There was a pause, and then, "I'll be wondering if your wrist has healed up yet? That's who I'll be."

Louise frowned warningly at her and intervened smoothly, "Good afternoon Mr Halverson. Allow me to introduce my colleague Miss Murray, owner of this establishment. I believe we've met before. I'm Mrs Pegram, head of Personnel."

A puzzled expression played over his face. "I don't think we've met before. I'm sure I would remember two such gracious ladies," he murmured emolliently, bowing slightly towards them, confident of his effect on middle-aged ladies.

"You weren't quite so polite last time we met." Miss Murray said baldly, unwilling to waste much time on the brash American. "You called us 'old dears,' then 'girls,' I think? Mrs Pegram, can you refresh my memory on that?" She turned to her friend, a small smile twitching at the corner of her mouth.

"Yes I'm afraid so Mr Halverson. Perhaps you remember your recent Hebridean holiday? We met in the little shop at Farbost on Shepsay. Not impressed by it we gathered."

"Not cut out for retail I think you said? Indeed? Well, Mr Halverson you'll no doubt be surprised to find that, somehow, we've been running all this for many years." She waved her arm to indicate the whole building.

He had the grace to look abashed and seemed temporarily lost for words. Then, "Gee I don't know what to say. I can't believe this is happening. I can only apologise. I guess I wasn't at my politest. I was in shock after that monster dog attacked me."

The ladies raised their eyebrows, monster dog indeed!

Margaret continued, "We never know when we'll come across a customer and can never risk being so rude to anyone. This is a prestigious store with customers all over Scotland and beyond.

"If you are inclined to such outbursts, then you cannot be seriously considered for employment by a business that sets such store on customer service and staff attitude."

He blustered, but was interrupted by Margaret as she continued, "I see from your application form that you have considerable experience in retail in New York. I worked there too in Bergdorf Goodman. You may have heard of it?" His eyes widened. She continued, "Yes, I too have considerable retail experience and in this experience I discovered that politeness to all was an absolute requisite for all staff at all times."

"Yes, yes of course," he gabbled. "It was a one-off event and I promise it will never happen again."

Remembering the incidents on the boat, Margaret dismissed his feeble protestations. Turning to Louise, she enquired, "Do we have any back room jobs vacant at present? Away from customers?"

Louise shook her head, ruefully aware that

Margaret had probably gone a bit too far. She turned her attention to the young man and said with finality, "It would seem that you are not compatible with any of the jobs in Murrays at present. It may be that you try for a job at Smedleys or some other place. But not here." She stood up and indicated that the interview was at an end. He walked out silently and they sat back as he slammed the door bad temperedly, going on to bang the heavy corridor door behind him as he left.

Margaret looked at Louise. "Gosh. I don't know what to say. If we hadn't met him before the chances are we would have employed him."

"A lucky escape then. Just like our holiday it would seem!"

Chapter 11

International Rescue

A chill wind was blowing metaphorically through the management meeting. Grim faced, Miss Murray passed round the letter she had received that morning. Personally addressed to her at her home, it was from Archie Smedley, proprietor of the great rival department store, Smedleys. Mr McElvey read it aloud to the others. It made for sad reading. Archie Smedley informed Miss Murray that, officially, Smedleys was for sale. They were forced into this due to disappearing revenue. Put plainly, they could no longer afford to trade. An offer had been received from a large chain, but Archie wondered if a merger or takeover by Murrays would be possible. Certainly, it would be preferable for him personally. He didn't want to "cast his long-term staff to the winds", as he put it.

The management team exchanged glances. Smedleys had been their trading competitor for as long as anyone could remember. The shop and its ethos was broadly similar to Murrays but, naturally, it was not nearly as good. They were all very sorry to hear of its demise. The implications for Murrays were stark. Would they be forced to go the same way? They were all aware that Smedleys had been running various cut-price sales for some time and that their window displays seemed to be moving further and further downmarket. Mr McElvey had previously voiced his suspicions, but he had been ignored as the voice of doom that he usually was.

There was silence for a while, then Miss Murray, who had been able to consider the letter and its suggestion for longer, spoke, "Well, what do you think? Could we buy them out? Would that be a good thing to do? Would it be financially possible?"

Mr McElvey shook his head vehemently. "We're in no position to do that I'm afraid. I keep a keen eye on the books as you all know." He looked at them all. They were nodding. He continued heavily, "In the trading year to date figures don't make for good reading I'm afraid. In fact, we're down in all departments."

Miss Murray looked alarmed. "Ian, you should have said…"

"No, no it's not that bad, we're not actually trading at," he paused, sighed, and said the words he most hated and feared, "a loss."

Miss Murray sat back relieved. "So we just can't buy them out? Okay. I'll tell him that. I'll write today." She changed her mind. "In fact, I'll take him out for lunch to tell him and maybe find out a bit more about the situation." They all agreed that would be a good approach. Mr McElvey offered to join her to 'talk turkey' as he called it. On balance, it was thought to be potentially useful if he did. The two began to discuss dates, times and venues for the event. As soon as possible seemed best.

At the next meeting, the team looked expectantly at Miss Murray and Mr McElvey, although they had all already been updated on the outcome of the lunch. No one had been able to wait and they were already aware that Smedleys as they knew it was gone. Now the task at hand for the Murrays management was to prevent such a future for their own 'department store of distinction.'

Mr Philipson didn't usually enter into the cut and thrust of typical arguments that tended to go on in meetings. He was a cheerful, outgoing person with a happy, busy family life. Unlike the others, work was just that to him: work. Nevertheless, he cared a great deal about Murrays and had been as appalled as everyone else about Smedleys. He was a cultural all-rounder who, despite being keen on sport, also enjoyed attending choral concerts, art exhibitions, plays and literary events with his extended family. He spoke up now.

"I've been thinking. There's a market we completely ignore and I think we could do well if we try to develop our offering to it."

"Really?" Mr McElvey was very interested.

"Go on," said Miss Murray.

"Well, it's just this. Edinburgh hosts the largest international arts festival in the world. It goes on around us every August and September and it seems to me that we just pretend it isn't happening."

"Well, it is very inconvenient," put in Mr Soames. "Tourists wander so slowly along, they just don't care that some of us actually have to get to work. They fill the buses and delay the drivers. Half the staff are late every day because of it."

Mrs Pegram had to agree.

"Well, rather than complain about it why don't we try to capitalise on it? Why don't we have a festival right here? In the store." The others looked at him blankly. He went on. "I've really been thinking about this. How about specialist food in the Food Hall, a puppet show in the Toy Department, fashion shows and so on? There's lots we could do. Lots of link-ups. How about offering space to the art college for art exhibitions?"

Miss Murray was very interested. "Oh yes," she said thoughtfully, "The walls of the Furniture Department are pretty bare; we could offer space there…" She was really keen now. "How about a fashion exhibition, you know Murrays' ladies through the ages sort of thing?"

"Yes of course. Brilliant. We'll need to get the staff involved of course. We could ask each department for suggestions." Mrs Pegram was on board too now. Everyone was nodding vehemently except Mr McElvey.

"It's a great risk of course."

"Is it? I don't see how. It won't cost us much except possibly in advertising." Miss Murray was puzzled.

"We risk alienating our core customers: the Edinburgh ladies. They already avoid coming into town during the festival."

"Good point. Maybe there's some sort of inducement we could offer though?" They all had a think.

"How about…" said Barry, who had been very quiet up till now as he considered the security implications of encouraging foreigners into the store, "…scones?"

"Scones?"

"Yes, we could offer free scones, or rather, a free scone to any account customer who brings in a guest? The guest doesn't have to be a foreigner, just a visitor. We could call it Murrays' welcome policy or something similar?"

"That could be difficult to police," said Mr McElvey, for whom offering free things was anathema. "But I see your point."

Barry was warming to his theme. "Then after the festival was over we could have a welcome *back* policy for the account holders who stayed away over the festival anyway."

"Well there's certainly a lot to think about," summed up Miss Murray, smiling at Mr Philipson in particular. "Excellent ideas all round. Let's progress this. We have a bit of time to organise it all. Louise, can you organise a memo to all departments outlining the plan and asking for their individual suggestions? Encourage them to be imaginative. You never know what good ideas people might have." Mrs Pegram nodded and said she'd get on it at once.

Mrs Pegram was as good as her word and a memo was circulated to each department asking them to think about how they might put on some sort of display or how they could reflect the international flavour of the season. This seemed to have the desired effect and the various departments were soon buzzing with ideas and suggestions. The buyers were asked to collate these and present them to Personnel for review and discussion by the management.

Looking at the large pile of notes that accrued from the departments it was obvious there was considerable enthusiasm for the project. Mrs Pegram shook her head in silent mirth at some of the wilder ideas: a circus in the Grand Hall, belly dancing in Ladies Lingerie or a hog roast in the Tea Room were unlikely to be taken up by the management. Their interest was noted and appreciated though. However, there were some useful ideas. The suggestion of daily puppet shows in the Toy Department, an art exhibition in the Furniture Department and play reading in the Bookshop were all considered doable.

Mrs Pegram and Miss Murray went round the various departments to discuss the suggestions. They waited politely in Hosiery while Mrs Garland and Susan served the short queue of customers. After all the ladies had left, each carrying small discreet parcels, Mrs Pegram began.

"Now Mrs Garland, I see you have suggested you wear a flamenco costume for the duration of the Festival. Is there any particular reason for this? Are you a dancer yourself perhaps?" she asked out of politeness rather than any genuine consideration that this was the case.

"No, no. I've just always wanted to wear one,"

Mrs Garland responded. "It's festive, isn't it?" she added defensively, "I thought you wanted something festive."

Susan moved forward to say something in her support but, before she could say anything, Mrs Garland moved her firmly aside, "Not now, Susan." Susan retreated.

"Well it certainly would be festive," Miss Murray said. "But I wonder what the customers might think. Would they, perhaps, expect that there would be a display of flamenco dancing in here?" She looked at the low-ceilinged Hosiery area and at the Ladies Lingerie Department that it led to. "Might it be rather confusing?"

"Well maybe," Mrs Garland conceded. Then, to everyone's surprise, including her own, Susan managed to interject.

"I could do Highland dancing. I've got all my medals for it and the costume." She lapsed into a sheepish silence. Mrs Garland glowered at her and she visibly quailed.

Mrs Pegram came to the rescue. "What an excellent idea! I had no idea you were harbouring such talent here Mrs Garland."

Mrs Garland bridled, keen to take the credit for her protégée's skills. "Well of course we don't want to make too much of it." She then began to see how it could all work.

"She could wear her Highland dancing outfit and I could wear my good white dress with a tartan sash," she added. "We could stock up on tartan tights and Scottish-type things to put on display."

"Excellent. Now you're talking," Miss Murray stoked her enthusiasm and turned to Susan, "Do you think you could do a display of Highland dancing? I bet we could find a piper among the staff." She looked enquiringly at Mrs Pegram.

"Yes, I believe one of the porters is a piper. He mentioned it at his interview. I don't know how good he is, but I'll try to find out. Would that be all right with you Susan?" Susan hung her head, abashed at her temerity, but secretly rather excited at the prospect of demonstrating her hitherto unsuspected skill. She nodded shyly. Mrs Garland, now sure it was entirely her idea, beamed at them all.

"Well that's settled. This is going to be fun."

"I just hope my fiancé Martin doesn't mind," Susan worried. "He really doesn't like change and disruption."

Moving on to the China and Glass Department, the two ladies were met by a rather breathless Eric Upton. He was aflame with enthusiasm for a pet project of his own. Despite Miss Piper's best efforts to subdue him, he persisted.

"Miss Murray I've had a brilliant idea." His eyebrows raised in hope.

Keen to encourage his eagerness, Mrs Pegram said, "Go on then, tell us." She threw a warning yet placatory glance at the outraged Miss Piper.

"Well it's this. You see my grandad was a

prisoner of war…"

"I'm sorry to hear that, but I don't quite see…" Miss Murray was puzzled.

"Well he was in a Highland Regiment. The Gordon Highlanders." He looked at her expectantly. She looked back blankly.

"The reel. The Reel of the 51st? Everyone knows about that." He looked defiantly at the ladies. Miss Piper tutted impatiently. Miss Murray shook her head, apologetic.

"Tell us more." Mrs Pegram rescued him.

"Well when the regiment was in this prisoner of war camp they invented a special Scottish country dance. It's called the Reel of the 51st. The main point is that the dancers form a large St Andrew's cross. The Germans didn't understand what was going on when the Colonel sent back the instructions to Scotland. They thought it was some sort of dangerous code! Hilarious."

The ladies were interested. "How would you see the China Department commemorating this?" Miss Murray said.

"We could dance it of course! My grandad could teach us all, and that piper, Ewan from the Porters could play for it. The right tune is 'The Drunken Piper'; I bet he knows it. We could do it no bother once we'd cleared all the china away," he continued hopefully.

"Ah. Well there's the snag I'm afraid," Miss Murray dashed his hopes as kindly as she could. "You see we're in business here. We need to have the stock available for sale." She gestured at the tables and display stands of china. She also wondered if the ageing floorboards could even take the jumping and thumping an enthusiastic reel would entail, however daintily they tried to perform it.

"But it's a lovely idea. I'm so interested to hear about it all."

Miss Piper cleared her throat.

"Miss Murray," she said, taking the conversational floor, "I've spoken to a couple of the manufacturers and they suggested sending up some china painters. Customers might like to see them at work? Then they might like to actually buy some items?" She looked triumphantly at the dejected Eric.

"What a good idea Miss Piper." Mrs Pegram was keen to support China and Glass, although she could see how crestfallen Eric was. "Don't worry Eric, there is going to be some Highland dancing and the piping porter will be involved." He shrugged his shoulders and, sighing, withdrew to the packing room to hide his disappointment. He knew Miss Piper would be having words with him about his pushiness after the ladies left.

Susan was quite accurate in her fears about Martin's reaction. Mr da Costa was very concerned about the disruption to his quiet, ordered department. Mrs Hope placated him by wondering how they could contribute to the festive atmosphere on his terms and, after a word with Mrs Pegram, a plan evolved which met with his approval. Unlike Ladies Separates, Ladies Outdoor Clothing and Casualwear, Model Gowns would not be providing a fashion show. They would have an exhibition of Model Gowns through the ages (or at least since Murrays had opened). Miss Murray recalled that all the best dresses belonging to the first, second and third Mrs Murray were safely stowed away in vast wardrobes in the attics of Rosehill. A dusty afternoon in a heady miasma of mothballs provided a treasure trove of fashionable garments from the nineteenth to the mid twentieth century. The big names were all represented as the various Mr Murrays had always insisted their wives' appearance reflected the very best of Murrays' fashionable clothing. There were dresses and costumes by Worth, Vionnet, Chanel and others; some dresses handmade in the workrooms of Murrays were also chosen and set up on models throughout the Model Gowns Department. Together with the appropriate hats, furs and accessories, the display was fabulous. Mr da Costa only hoped that the department wouldn't be invaded by "inappropriate ladies" as he put it, meaning those unlikely to afford the prices. These hopes were to be swiftly dashed.

And so the preparations continued. Department after department came up with ideas great and small to reflect an overall impression that Murrays was running a festival of its very own. The Tea Room was braced to provide the required scones. Although this was only after prolonged negotiations with Mr McElvey and agreement that the free scones would be slightly smaller than usual and resolutely plain only. No cheese or fruit scone was to be provided free of charge and there was to be no question of jam.

As the festival drew near, there was a discernible feeling of excitement throughout the store. Even those staff who did not have direct contact with customers felt the change in the air. In the staff canteen, Mrs Collins gave herself permission to be rather more experimental with her cuisine than usual and her Spaghetti Bolognese was widely considered to be an improvement on the usual pasta dishes. Usually, she only offered macaroni.

When the festival officially opened and tourists flooded the city, the increased alertness and enthusiasm among the staff was immediately noticeable to the customers who began to visit the store in larger and larger numbers. The scone enticement to local customers also paid dividends and, week on week, the sales takings increased markedly. Customers from abroad, mostly American, but Europeans too, really liked the store itself. Various conversations were held between these visitors and individual staff members and positive relationships were forged. Many of the new customers resolved to return to the store and most certainly to tell their friends and families about the Scottish store where they enjoyed whiling away many hours (and dollars) while enjoying dance displays, art exhibitions and various other cultural events. The display of Model Gowns through the ages was heavily photographed and several glossy magazines featured it in their autumn editions. For the most part, the images of Mr da Costa glowering in the background were edited out.

After the festival finally petered out, and the city returned to some form of normality, the management team convened to review the final figures and discuss the outcome of the project.

"Well, first of all, congratulations to Mr Philipson on his excellent idea," opened Miss Murray. "It's all gone so well. I couldn't be more pleased. The whole store seemed energised and it looks like the figures have been supercharged!"

She smiled towards Mr McElvey who grudgingly nodded, then started dolorously, "That's all very well but of course our problem now is how to maintain these sales levels. We're bound to slump before Christmas and then have to sell off the excess stock in the January sales."

There was silence, then Mrs Pegram spoke up, "I've been talking to Mr Morrison in Display and Advertising and he's had a good idea." The others looked expectantly at her. "Well, basically, we've had so many direct export sales when customers from abroad have arranged for us to send their newly purchased goods direct to their homes, that we now have a huge directory of the home addresses of overseas customers. How about we really develop our, what he called, 'off site sales'? We could do a beefed-up catalogue and make it part of a direct marketing campaign, an international campaign capitalising on all our new customers?"

"Gosh," said Miss Murray, sitting back in her seat reflectively. "That could be terrific. Would it be expensive to set up?"

"Not necessarily," cut in Mr Soames. "The advertising department can design and produce the catalogues and letters etcetera and we could look at creating a special link between potential mail order sales and administration, item retrieval and the packing department. It's all there. We've just got to do a little work on the reconfiguration."

"Postage of all these catalogues will be expensive," put in Mr McElvey.

"Yes, but try to look on it as an investment." Miss Murray had already made up her mind.

"This sounds like a very specific project. We would need to study what changes have to be made and pull it all into shape with Display and Advertising to carry it through. Who should we put in charge of it? We'll need some fresh ideas and Mr Morrison can steer it generally."

"Well, naturally Samantha would be ideal," suggested Mr McElvey.

"Yes, good idea, she's got your head for figures Ian," Miss Murray agreed, then looked at Mrs Pegram enquiringly. "Do you have anyone in particular in mind?"

"I was wondering about Anjali Joshi," she

started. "She's such a bright girl and she's done her time in Floristry. She made some excellent suggestions for improvements there and despite that she still got on well with everyone in the department. I was just wondering where she could be placed next."

"Oh yes. Those two could work together very well. I like it. Is everyone agreed? It's a great project for them to get their teeth into. Good training too. This could be a real development for Murrays." Miss Murray was very enthusiastic. She could see new avenues opening up for Murrays just when they might need them most. The demise of Smedleys cast a long shadow.

"Now, back to business. The welcome back project. Who'd like to spearhead that? It's time to tempt our account customers back now the festival is over."

"Not more free scones." Mr McElvey groaned. The others sighed and shook their heads at him.

Back in her office, a wide smile spread across Mrs Pegram's face. Well, fancy that! Murrays were thinking big and thinking far away. She was in exactly the right place at the right time. She was where she was needed. She was staying at Murrays.

Looking vaguely upwards, she mentally called out, "Thank you, Iain Pegram."

Chapter 12

An Emergence

The management corridor was on the same floor as the staff canteen. The entrances to both led from the same staircase, but there the resemblance ended. Where the canteen featured tiled walls, often streaming with condensation, the management corridor was wood panelled with bevelled glass doors leading from it. The floor in the management corridor was covered in good quality but not extravagant carpeting laid on the orders of (very) old Mr Murray. The floor in the canteen was of unapologetic linoleum. The landing at the top of the stairs leading to the fifth floor was thus a no man's land between Murrays' management and staff.

The canteen, despite its depressing décor, was generally a cheerful place. It was uncertain whether this was due to the food or the respite it provided from work in Murrays' various departments. The sound of staff conversation rose and fell in volume throughout the day depending on the meal break in question. Between 9.30 and 11.30am there was a gradually increasing hum as the first break was taken in relays. From 11.30am till 1.30pm, the noise level rose again as lunch took place, then there was quiet until the afternoon breaks began at 2.30pm. After 4pm it changed again and a blessed silence reigned.

Four pm was Mrs Collins' favourite time of day. She could sit down, have a cigarette and go over the food orders for the next few days, checking there was enough of all the provisions to fulfil the not very adventurous menu. She often longed to make more exciting food, but there had been disasters and since the dreadful day of the goat curry she restricted herself to the perennial favourites such as macaroni or the eponymous cauliflower au gratin *with cheese*. She still felt strongly that it was not food poisoning as such that had had such an effect on the staff, but instead a sort of mass hysteria that had led to soaring levels of absence after the fateful curry. Mrs Pegram had been sympathetic, but strongly encouraged her to stick to the old favourites. Mrs Collins reluctantly agreed.

This afternoon Mrs Collins went through to the store room. Geographically, it lay between the canteen and the management corridor, but could only be accessed via a door at the back of the canteen kitchen. Being windowless, it was dark until the light was switched on. Shelves stretched around three walls and large metal bins and sagging cardboard containers were kept on the floor against the other wall.

It is a sad, or at least uncomfortable, fact that where there is food there also tends to be creatures other than humans feeding on it. In this case, whenever the light was switched on, brownish cockroaches could be seen scuttling for cover. Mrs Collins was quite accustomed to this and, depending on her mood, stamped on them wildly.

Today she unthinkingly took out six. She

sometimes wondered about mice. Did they keep down cockroaches or vice versa? Absent mindedly, she registered that there seemed to be fewer cockroaches these days and certainly no mice at all. Unusually for a cook, she quite liked mice; she liked most animals. In the interests of hygiene and keeping her job she did set traps for the mice, but always got Jim the porter to dispose of the tiny bodies.

As she examined her list and crossed off or added items as appropriate, she became aware of a slight movement from one of the boxes on the floor. Shaking her head a little she decided she'd had too much coffee that day as she had a slight headache. Five minutes later, more obviously, a small sound came from within the box. It really could not be ignored. In some trepidation, and wondering whether to call for someone else, she opened the cardboard flap at the top of the box. She peered inside, hesitantly at first and then much more enthusiastically; peering straight back at her were a pair of crystal blue eyes set in a mass of chocolate brown fur and cream coloured whiskers. The little creature emitted a small, polite miaow.

"Hello," she said. "Who are you then? What on earth are you doing in my store room?"

The little cat yawned, stretched and delicately jumped out of the box. It leaned companionably against Mrs Collins' legs.

"Oh, you are just so beautiful!" she exclaimed gathering it up in her arms. The little cat made no objection to being handled like this, but struggled awkwardly as Mrs Collins ascertained that the cat was a female. Regaining her dignity, the little creature allowed herself to be cuddled. Mrs Collins was a confirmed cat lover and knew just how to hold her. The little cat purred quietly.

"What are we going to do with you?" Mrs Collins asked plaintively. "You can't stay here, really you can't."

The cat looked back at her unconcernedly. Secure in her beauty, she was quite sure that she would be looked after and all would be well. The end of the working day was rapidly approaching and Mrs Collins couldn't think what to do with her new friend. Registering that doors downstairs were closing noisily and lights were being switched off as staff called out loud goodnights, she made a snap decision.

"You stay here tonight gorgeous, and I'll think of something in the morning." She quickly put out a saucer of milk and some leftover stovies and apologetically left the store room saying, "Night-night," as she went.

The little cat responded with a small goodnight miaow.

The next morning Mrs Collins arrived at work earlier than usual. Registering this, Mr Timmins the caretaker asked her anxiously "You're early today Mrs Collins. Not planning anything special in the canteen I hope?"

She shook her head impatiently. Mr Timmins

was one of those who had apparently suffered food poisoning following the curry. She carried on upstairs, panting slightly as she approached the fifth floor. Quickly crossing to the canteen kitchen, she was appalled to see that the store room door was ajar. Opening it and calling out "Puss, puss," she entered to find that the little cat had gone. She panicked, rushing round the kitchen and canteen looking for her new friend, but to no avail. Her mind reeling, she was just wondering what to do next when she heard a loud cry. It came from the open door to the staircase. The cry was of such distress that, without thinking, she rushed towards it, crossed the landing and entered the management corridor.

A door was open, framing a thin angular figure who seemed frozen in place.

"Mr McElvey, are you alright sir?" said Mrs Collins, rushing forward.

"Look," he spat. She inched around him and looked into his office. There, settled comfortably on the chair behind his desk, was the little cat. She blinked endearingly at Mrs Collins, then slowly stood up, stretched luxuriously and daintily stepped up onto Mr McElvey's desk. Seeing her fully for the first time, it became clear that this was no ordinary cat. She had a chocolate brown face, legs and tail, but her body was beige in colour and she had four perfectly white feet. This was striking enough, but her bright sparkling blue eyes were quite stunning. As though fully aware of her effect on people, she sat down and began a comprehensive bath, her little pink tongue rasping over her paws as she delicately completed her toilette.

Mr McElvey, at length moving forward into the office, stood aghast, emitting half syllables. "What the... how... who?"

Following him in, Mrs Collins began, "Oh Mr McElvey I can explain..." before realising that she actually couldn't. By this time other members of the management team began to arrive. Doors could be heard opening all down the corridor.

Mrs Carr burst in officiously and then came to an abrupt halt. "A cat? In Mr McElvey's office? Get it out, get it out at once." she screeched, looking accusingly at Mrs Collins.

"No wait." Mr McElvey surprised them. He appeared transfixed by the lovely little creature. He stepped forward and stretched out a hesitant hand towards the cat. She stood up and arched her head into his hand. Unexpectedly, he began to stroke her between the ears and round the side of her head ending up by tickling her under her chin. The little cat revelled in this and began to purr loudly. Mr McElvey smiled. A rare event.

"Coffee I think Mrs Carr if you please," he said as he walked to his chair and sat down behind his desk.

He reached out to the little cat again and she obligingly leaned in towards him.

"She really likes you, sir." Mrs Collins ventured at last. "Well I'd better be on my way. I'll need to get things going in the kitchen." She said this as she backed out of the room, half expecting to be called back. Mr McElvey nodded and looked around for today's post. He opened the top drawer of his desk to look for a notebook and the cat stepped straight into it and sat down tidily. Mr McElvey laughed quietly then applied himself to dealing with the day's mail.

When Miss Murray popped her head around the door an hour later, she was amazed at the scene in front of her: the starchy Mr McElvey was leaning over his notes while a little cat, sitting in a drawer next to him, serenely observed the scene.

Miss Murray tiptoed out and knocked on Mrs Pegram's door.

"Come quick Louise, you've got to see this," she hissed.

Mrs Pegram took in the urgency of her statement, but also noted the twitch in her friend's mouth. *Whatever was going on must be amusing she thought.* The two ladies knocked and entered Mr McElvey's room. Mrs Pegram could not hold back, "Ian! What's going on? Who's your friend?"

Miss Murray laughed, "Oh yes you must introduce us."

"Well she um, she was just here this morning when I came in." he replied. "She's a nice little thing. Very friendly. She's a girl I gather," he faltered.

"Where on earth did you get her?" queried Mrs Pegram.

"I didn't, I didn't *get* her myself. She was just here this morning. Here, sitting on my seat nice as you like." He began to stroke the little cat again.

"Well I never," burst out Miss Murray. "I never thought I'd see you coming round to the delights of feline companionship."

She continued to laugh, to Mr McElvey's growing irritation.

Ever practical, Mrs Pegram continued, "Well she must have come from somewhere."

"Mrs Collins, the lady from the canteen, seemed to know something I think, why not ask her?" he replied, very obviously going back to his work.

"Right. I'll do that." Feeling dismissed, Mrs Pegram left the room and set off across the corridor towards the canteen. Still smiling, Miss Murray returned to her office.

Mrs Collins couldn't offer any explanation for the cat's sudden emergence either. The two women looked at each other in some concern. "She's obviously a pedigree of some sort. She looks like a Birman. I once saw one at a cat show. They're very unusual."

"And beautiful too if this one is anything to go by. What are we going to do with her though?" said Mrs Pegram, "She must belong to someone. I'll put the word out round the departments and see if anyone knows where she came from. In the meantime, we'll need to make some arrangements for her, if you know what I mean Mrs Collins?" She nodded meaningfully. Mrs Collins knew at once what Mrs Pegram was talking about and reassured her as to the litter tray she had set up in a discreet corner. She had also sent one of the juniors out to buy some cat food.

In time the most probable history of the little cat's arrival emerged. It transpired that a recent consignment of Persian rugs had arrived in the Carpet Department on the floor below. The rugs had been brought overland from Antalya via Paris by a family of enterprising carpet dealers. Mr Joshi had caught sight of a cream-coloured flash out of the corner of his eye as he opened one of the large boxes of rugs. But he had been concentrating on the contents of the box, keen to check that the rugs were of the promised quality. It was likely that at some point in the journey the little cat had seen an open box and, being a cat, jumped in and settled down happily. Now far from home, the little stowaway had jumped out and hidden as the boxes of rugs were being opened. She must have been frightened and hidden herself until the shop closed for the night; then she went exploring, her nose leading her to the food store cupboard in the kitchen. In the morning something had attracted her to Mr McElvey's office. Certainly, she had walked past several other offices before she got to his and decided to settle on his chair.

The sudden emergence of the cat was the first topic of the next morning's management meeting. By that time Mrs Collins had taken her to a local vet where she was pronounced fit and well.

Everyone was surprised when Mr McElvey refunded the costs for this visit from petty cash without demur. He even pressed Mrs Collins to return and ask whether quarantine was to be thought of. The vet, a practical man, considered the problem. The cat could have entered the box, if indeed that was how she arrived at Murrays, at any point between Turkey and Edinburgh, including several stops in England. Under the circumstances, he felt that as she was patently in good health, although slightly thin, a quarantine cattery wasn't called for. When this was relayed to them, everyone's relief was palpable.

Over the next week the likeable little creature had a remarkable effect on store morale. She spent her time on the top floor between the canteen and the management corridor and was very popular with all. The uncertainty of her nationality added a certain cachet to her already glamorous appearance. She appeared to understand English, although perhaps that was going a bit too far as murmured endearments, such as she was almost universally subjected to, didn't necessarily require translation. She would patrol the tables in the canteen during breaks and graciously accepted snacks from her new fans. She was a great attraction. On several occasions, when the cat was not to be found in the canteen, a flustered Miss Manson from Linens was discovered on her hands and knees whispering, "Puss, Puss," at the door to the management corridor in the hope of enticing her furry friend out for a cuddle.

Even Mr Timmins, a notorious hater of cats, developed a grudging liking for her when she demonstrated an unexpected skill as a mouser. Mr McElvey became the unhappy recipient of at least a brace of mice each morning.

Mrs Pegram was keen to formalise the situation and brought the subject up at a management meeting. "She can sleep in the canteen cupboard if she wants to, generally making her presence felt overnight among the rodent population, and she can stay with Mr McElvey in his office during the day," she said. "We'll need to put her on the payroll to pay for her keep and vets bills etc. We'll also need to find her a name. Any ideas anyone?" She looked expectantly at the team members around the table. The creature in question was sitting blissfully happily in a sunbeam on the wooden windowsill behind Mr McElvey. The painted Mr Murrays in their lavish gilt frames looked on with stern disapproval.

"She's such a beautiful little thing," ventured Miss Murray, "vaguely oriental somehow."

Mr McElvey agreed. He was a great admirer of Gilbert and Sullivan and had recently attended the first night of that season's Mikado. "I've got it," he called out enthusiastically, "how about YumYum?"

Barry Hughes, attending this meeting to discuss security matters, agreed. "Yes. She certainly looks good enough to eat."

Mr McElvey blanched. "What on earth do you

mean man?"

He was not familiar with the range of sticky pastries to which Barry referred.

Blustering, Barry explained his thinking.

Miss Murray and Mrs Pegram nodded at each other. "I think that's settled then" said Miss Murray and turned to the little cat, "Hello, YumYum."

YumYum blinked calmly, yawned, stretched and went to sleep.

Chapter 13

Toxicity

Miss Eleanor McFarlane ran a tight ship. The 'HMS' Food Hall at Murrays was famed for its wide variety of food and drink. Hailing from all nations, each item was of unimpeachable quality and beauty of appearance. Chocolates from Belgium came in exquisite boxes, smoked salmon from chilly Scottish rivers was displayed to advantage in tartan trimmed cold cabinets, and wine and spirits bottles sparkled and winked in the lighting above their mahogany display shelves.

The produce in the Food Hall was the best of the best and the steep prices reflected this, as did Miss McFarlane herself.

Miss McFarlane was tall and slim to the point of frailty. Perfectly turned out at all times, her hair and make-up were subtly advantageous, and her clothes tailored to fit as though sewn by the best of couturiers. Striking though the image she presented was, it was her voice that most caught the attention. She spoke with what used to be called a 'cut-glass accent' or, more colloquially, as though she had 'bools in the mooth.' This added to her mystique as many naturally assumed that she came from a titled background or was even a (minor) member of royalty.

Despite her appearance and manner of vague charm to customers and management, this charm was not apparent to her workers. Miss McFarlane was a harsh taskmaster with very high standards. She was very strict with her staff and unforgiving of any mistake, however small.

Mrs Pegram regularly dealt with tearful ex-members of the Food Hall staff seeking re-appointment to another department. She discussed this at the management meeting one day. "Miss McFarlane's done it again," she opened. "That young Mr Pearson seems to have blotted his copy book and been summarily sacked."

Miss Murray was interested. "What's he done? He seemed a promising young man?" she asked.

"He mixed up the baking on display and made the hideous mistake of labelling Kaiser Rolls as Granary Assorted Rolls I gather."

"Is that all? Surely anyone can make a wee mistake like that," queried Mr Philipson.

"I know," replied Mrs Pegram, "but I gather that this would, and I quote, 'lead to our customers making erroneous choices to their severe disadvantage.'" This was said in an accurate imitation of Miss McFarlane's accent. They all smiled in recognition.

"Well, I'm all for high standards but this is a bit ridiculous," Miss Murray continued. "Have you been able to fit Mr Pearson in somewhere else?"

"Oh yes. Electricals were needing someone and he's nice and tall... He can reach the light fittings," she explained in answer to puzzled frowns.

This brought nods of agreement from around

the table and the team moved on to other agenda items.

Miss McFarlane was not without support in her life's work of maintaining high standards in the Food Hall. Her assistant, Miss Butters, had worked alongside her for many years. Miss Butters was the antithesis of Miss McFarlane; she was small, rounded to the point of tubbiness and her flyaway hair and rather untidy appearance rendered her a figure of fun among younger members of staff. Her smudged spectacles and down at heel shoes were frequently commented on.

The staff could never understand why the immaculate Miss McFarlane favoured Miss Butters. However, favour her she did, and Miss Butters basked in her senior's approval despite her dishevelled appearance. Popular opinion was that Miss Butters acted as a conduit between Miss McFarlane and the staff, thus reducing the actual time she had to directly deal with them. The Food Hall staff were glad of this as many had quailed at Miss McFarlane's tone of voice when speaking to them. Miss Butters, the go-between, had known Miss McFarlane for many years and knew all her preferences as to paperwork completion, ordering quotas and display options. She was the only member of staff that Miss McFarlane trusted to cover her rare absences. She could be relied upon to agree with Miss McFarlane at all times and on all matters. Needless to say, the staff hated her too. The two women were referred to disparagingly behind their backs as 'Her Ladyship' and 'Marge.'

Unsurprisingly, the atmosphere in the Food Hall was not good. Morale was very low indeed. Such staff as remained in employment considered that they held onto their jobs by the skin of their teeth and always felt as though they were "treading on eggshells," as one said to another.

Miss McFarlane and Miss Butters had worked together for years, and worked was the word for it. Unsuspected by the management team and most staff, Miss McFarlane was quite prepared to roll up her lacy sleeves and work every bit as hard as her workforce. She was first in the loading bay as consignments of rare fruit were delivered, even going so far as to clamber into the backs of the delivery lorries and inspect the cargoes before they were offloaded. She would fetch and carry heavy wine boxes and climb up ladders to high shelves to display exotic tins of virgin olive oil or unusual liqueurs. After a session of such hard physical labour and a quick visit to the Ladies Room, she was restored to her usual pristine self.

Miss Butters knew this and respected her for it. She was especially impressed that her manner never changed and she was as icily polite to members of staff as she dismissed them as she was to customers searching for a particular delicacy.

Perhaps surprisingly, Miss McFarlane was very popular with the customers. They felt that she added a real touch of class to the Food Hall and some insisted on dealing only with her. She was often consulted regarding catering for social events and frequently graced them herself. Even the less well-off customers appreciated being served by her; they were glad she understood that some people would rather have one really nice item than six lesser ones. Her policy of selling scones in small packets of two, or single cream cakes, was a popular one and many proudly carried home their small delicacy in a Murrays bag. However, Miss McFarlane infinitely preferred her more socially prominent customers to the little women in their best coats buying a wee treat for later.

It was in relation to one of these socially prominent customers (or "posh yins" as Miss Butters called them) that the latest staff member had fallen foul of Miss McFarlane. Young Darren Smith was an enthusiastic new recruit. He had told Mrs Pegram in his interview that he had always wanted to work at Murrays. Blinking at her through his spectacles, he had confided breathily that he "Fair liked the Food Hall," and wondered, "What would ma chances be of a job there?"

Mrs Pegram was a little surprised that he aspired to the Food Hall but was uncomfortably aware that it had yet another vacancy. She looked at him speculatively. He would need to smarten up; Miss McFarlane would not allow him in her department dressed as he was in a too tight brown suit with an obviously grubby collar. The tie would have to go too, she thought, or at least the egg on it. However, it was refreshing to meet such a keen young man. It was a pity he was so obviously overweight. She brightened as she thought that after all it was the Food Hall: he could be seen as a good advertisement for their delicious wares. She smiled as she stood up and shook his hand. "Welcome to Murrays," she said. "The Food Hall it is. You can start on Monday."

The next Monday a visibly nervous Darren presented himself in the Food Hall. Miss McFarlane, far from welcoming the new recruit, glanced briefly at him, grimaced, and sent him to wash his hands.

"Too, too filthy," she called out over her shoulder as she stalked off to inspect and deplore a new delivery of "imperfect" handmade chocolates.

Darren looked at his feet in embarrassment, then around him at the others who had gathered to welcome the latest victim.

"Welcome to the Food Hall. It's always like this by the way," said Mrs Clark, a mouse-like person of relative longstanding (ten months) in the department.

"Oh, er, right." Darren stammered. "Where shall I...?" he faltered, wondering where to wash his hands.

"This way son," said Miss Butters (Marge) grimly and led him off to the hand basin in the backroom. The others looked after them and shrugged their shoulders. "Well, he won't last long," was the general consensus. They returned silently to their various tasks.

The chastened Darren returned soon after and, at Miss Butter's direction, he set to work turning all the tins and bottles around on their shelves so that their labels faced the front. He concentrated so hard on this task, with his tongue protruding slightly as he mouth-breathed, that he kept steaming up his glasses and having to stop to polish them on his tie. No one thought to tell him when he could take a break so he continued doggedly for several hours. He began following customers around, rapidly rearranging any stock item that they may have picked up to examine more closely. He didn't seem to notice the irritated glances he was receiving as he followed, hot on their heels, breathing loudly.

Miss McFarlane, in conversation with a customer vehemently outlining her preference for Beluga as opposed to Sevruga Caviar, observed Lady Harrison, a favoured customer, walk briskly out of the department after a few sharp words to Darren.

"Oh, I do entirely agree with you," she purred to her customer, "For me it's Beluga all the way." Then, "do excuse me." She moved smoothly over to Darren, a pleasant smile on her face for the benefit of passing customers.

"What was all that about?" she hissed. Taking in his rumpled and distasteful appearance, she continued, "Oh for God's sake what do you look like? You're a disgrace. A complete disgrace. I don't know what Mrs Pegram was thinking of. I've seen smarter more intelligent monkeys than you!"

Darren gasped at this and his eyes filled with

tears, which were much magnified by his glasses. He mumbled and sniffed unappealingly. Miss Butters, attracted by the appearance of an altercation, had arrived in time to hear Miss McFarlane's comments. Miss McFarlane told her what she'd seen. Darren tried his best to interject that he was just trying to do as he'd been told, but he was completely ignored by Miss McFarlane. Miss Butters looked on as Darren was told to collect his things at once. His days, or rather his half day, in the Food Hall was over. With a last despairing sniff, he withdrew to the cloakroom, collected his grubby jacket, and departed from Murrays. Miss MacFarlane raised her eyebrows in mock horror at Miss Butters and set off after Lady Harrison. A good customer like that had to be retrieved and ruffled feathers smoothed.

The management team, to their discredit, laughed to hear of the shortest ever employment in the Food Hall. "So far," added Mrs Pegram darkly.

She had telephoned the young man at home to ascertain his side of the story and offer him a job working with the porters. He accepted this offer with touching gratitude.

And so life went on in the Food Hall. The seasons came and went, reflected by fluctuations in the stock: the Christmas and Easter specialities, the appearance and disappearance of soft fruits, cheeses and pâtés, as supplies waxed and waned.

Profit margins were maintained and occasionally exceeded and all went well until the fateful day of the letter.

It arrived, no one knew how, on Miss Murray's desk. Hand written and addressed "To whom it may concern." Miss Murray was certainly concerned, especially once she had read what was neatly written on the single sheet of paper that it contained:

You'd better find the poison in the Food Hall before a customer does.

Miss Murray blanched and fumbled blindly for the phone.

The hastily assembled management team discussed the note in anxious tones. Mr Soames wanted to call the Police or the Public Health Inspectors at once, but this was rapidly vetoed as they considered the potential effect it could have on sales.

"Customers could avoid us completely if word got out," said Mrs Pegram.

"And it would get out," added Mr McElvey sourly, "and they would never come back." He continued, shaking his head. He was a glass half empty sort of person.

Mr Philipson, a glass half full man, put forward a more cheerful option, "It's a joke, just a joke. No one could really mean it." They mulled this over doubtfully.

"It's no use. We have to do something," said Miss Murray who only believed in the wrong size of glass. "We simply cannot risk anyone being poisoned by something bought from Murrays' Food Hall."

"We'll need to close the Food Hall at least temporarily." Mr Soames said, stung by his first suggestion being so summarily dismissed.

"Yes, that's quite right. Phone down and get the Food Hall doors closed off. Say it's for decoration or Health and Safety checks or something in the meantime." Miss Murray took charge. "Let's get Miss McFarlane up here and call Barry Hughes to come in too. This is a security matter."

Half an hour later, the team had arranged for the Food Hall to be closed for "repairs" according to the smart new notice produced by Display and Advertising, staff had been dispersed to other departments and deliveries of fresh produce diverted. Disappointed regular customers made their way out of the shop, complaining as they went. Barry, observing this, thought about their lucky escape; they could be complaining about much more than not having their usual brand of smoked salmon pâté. He'd had food poisoning before and it certainly wasn't pleasant. He grimaced as he remembered it.

Back in the boardroom, a distraught Miss McFarlane and a more than usually dishevelled Miss Butters looked wordlessly at Miss Murray. They scanned the note and Miss McFarlane had to sit down. Her shock was palpable. She trembled and her teeth chattered. She tried to speak but only half syllables were emitted.

Eventually, Miss Butters put their combined

thoughts into words: "Thon's awfy." She pronounced slowly.

Miss McFarlane looked up at her, still standing, and smiled gratefully.

Collecting herself visibly, Miss McFarlane rose to the occasion. "We must clear the shelves of all perishables and closely examine all and any sealed containers, bottles or tins." She stood up, ready to begin a battle against this unseen and dangerous enemy.

"Not so fast, Miss McFarlane," began Barry, keen to use his self-reported detective skills. "Why has this happened? Why would anyone want to cause such havoc?" He had been reading the latest newspaper and continued, "Is it political by any chance? Have you been buying in stock from some country with a nasty human rights policy?"

Her Ladyship shook her well-bred head nervously, "I don't know, I don't think so. Can you think of anything like that Miss Butters?" Obviously flustered, she turned to her ally.

"Well that last batch of shortbread came from Northern Ireland," Marge ventured cautiously, "Some of the ladies weren't too happy that we didn't stock good Scottish shortie."

"I can't see typical Murrays ladies going to such lengths over imported biscuits." Barry replied impatiently, then turned his, purely imaginary, laser-like attention towards Miss Murray, "or could this be someone striking a blow against Murrays itself? This could cost thousands of pounds in destruction of stock or even tens of thousands if a customer is poisoned. The adverse publicity could close the shop," he continued, oblivious to Miss Murray's increasing distress.

Miss Murray swallowed nervously. "I don't think I could be accused of having done anything to upset anyone…" she started. "But then it could be anyone that had a grudge against any department, anyone at all." She sighed unhappily, wondering who or why anyone would want to carry out such an act against Murrays.

She had a terrifying thought – could it be a competitor? Her thoughts turned darkly towards the new owners of Smedleys, Murrays' long-term rivals. Was this the start of a dirty tricks campaign with the aim of another aggressive takeover bid? Her mind reeled at the possibilities.

For the first time she felt her age. The day had started so well and now this: the store and its future, catapulted into uncertainty.

Meanwhile, a sudden thought occurred to Barry about the letter itself, "How exactly did this arrive? In the post? There's no stamp."

"It was just on my blotter when I came in this morning. It was in the internal mail pile."

Barry picked up on this excitedly, "Oho, so it's an inside job then?" he asked of no one in particular. "Right. I'm off to Mr Timmins to check on who has been posting what in the internal mail box and who sorts it into individual piles etc." He turned on his heel eagerly and left the room. The others looked at each other. Miss Murray was near to tears with a combination of shock and dismay.

Miss McFarlane and Miss Butters returned forlornly to the now unoccupied Food Hall to look listlessly and accusingly at their beloved stock. No order had yet been given to clear the shelves. Miss McFarlane picked up various of the more perishable items. Could this be a puncture mark in a packet of smoked salmon? Was this loaf of speciality bread unusually heavy? Might this jar's lid be a little loose? She speculated endlessly on how exactly or where precisely the poison could be placed, looking around hopelessly. Marge made soothing noises but couldn't think what to do. All the familiar routines of life in the Food Hall had evaporated. Outside the closed doors they could clearly hear disappointed customers vociferously expressing their displeasure at the closure of their favourite department. The two women sighed and huddled together for comfort. It was a sad scene.

After his visit to the caretaker to discuss the internal mail, Barry went up to the canteen, "to have a think," as he put it to himself. In reality he wanted to discuss the matter with his friend Jock the lift operator. He tried to play it cool, or so he thought.

"So Jock, old boy. Busy morning. Can't say much. Top Secret, hush hush and all that," he tapped the side of his nose.

Jock interrupted him, "Is it about the Food Hall?" he asked. "One of the ladies in my lift was saying it was closed."

"Possibly, possibly," continued Barry loftily, then relented. He had to discuss it with someone. Jock had always been discreet, besides which he was his only friend. He outlined the facts so far: the arrival of the note, the closure of the Food Hall and the fact that the note was, as confirmed by Mr Timmins, in the internal mail. No one unexpected had been seen to place any letters for internal distribution. "So it could have been any member of staff at all," he exclaimed in frustration. "I don't know what to do next." He looked at Jock hopefully. Jock continued chewing his bacon roll, but indicated that he was considering what he had heard.

Eventually, Jock offered, "Well the Food Hall itself isn't very popular with staff. Could it be from a disgruntled ex-employee? Trying to make trouble? Mrs Pegram seems to keep people on if she can after they've left Her Ladyship's department. Could one of them be getting their own back on Miss McFarlane?"

Barry looked doubtful, he didn't want to show that he hadn't actually thought of that. "Well it's a long shot but I suppose I could look into it," he responded wearily. This plan had the added benefit of an excuse to see Mrs Pegram for whom he had yearned at a distance for years. She repeatedly rejected his invitations, but he still entertained hopes in her direction. These were undoubtedly wasted hopes, but he had never accepted this. "I'll pop up and see old Louise after I've finished this," he said, gulping his still red hot coffee down. Coughing slightly as he stood up, he called, "See you later. Are you on first or second lunch today?" but barely waited for a response in his headlong rush to the Personnel Department. Jock, looking after him, shook his head ruefully. *When will he learn*, he thought.

Mrs Pegram looked doubtfully at Barry.

"An inside job?" she queried, "Do you really think it could be?" She had also wondered if it was a warning shot in a takeover battle. She had heard of such things. If it was, it didn't bode well for Murrays that the new owners of Smedleys were prepared to stoop to such tactics. Times were beginning to tell for large independent department stores. However, the nature of the threat seemed so personal. Poison pen letters were a very feminine sort of threat. Not the sort of activity of a large commercial organisation. She realised that they were all becoming overstressed and wildly thinking up possible reasons. Barry's suggestion seemed, improbably, to be quite a useful one. She considered the list of the most recent departures from the Food Hall. Of the last eight, five had been re-employed. Two ladies to Haberdashery and one man each to Furnishings, Electricals and the Porters. The three who had left altogether were employed in varying capacities at other, lesser, shops. She passed this on to Barry.

"Thanks Louise, that gives me something to work on," he breezed. "While I'm here I don't suppose..." he looked at her hopefully.

Sensing what was coming, she cut in, "Er, no Barry, I don't think so," before he could continue with his invitation to join him for a light dinner at The Golden Egg.

Barry made his way down to Haberdashery. Located in the basement of the shop, it was a destination of necessity rather than a place that needed to tempt customers. Reels of elastic, sewing requisites, safety pins, tapestry wool, buttons and zips were the staples. It was a relatively busy department, but not a very exciting one to work in. The two ladies behind the counter were busy with customers but another woman was just visible behind the stock room curtain reading a magazine with obvious enjoyment, her lips moving as she scanned each line. Clearly, the head of that department was off or on her break otherwise such slackness would never be tolerated.

Barry tiptoed up to her then loudly enquired what her name was. In a flurry she dropped the flimsy magazine and looked up, angry at being disturbed. "What do you want?" she asked rudely.

"You may not know me but I'm Mr Hughes, Head of Security, and I might ask you what you were doing young lady?" He could see at once that she was exactly the sort of person that wouldn't have lasted long under Miss McFarlane's iron rule.

"I'm Sonia Halliday," she sniffed and continued cheekily, "And I don't see what that's got to do with security."

"I'll be the judge of that." Barry snapped, quite taken aback at her attitude. He didn't think she'd last long at Murrays at all. However, looking at her and listening to her tone he somehow couldn't see her as the sort of person who would go to such energetic lengths as writing and sending a poison pen letter to the Managing Director. "You used to work in the Food Hall I gather," he continued.

"Yes. What of it? I hated it there and that's the truth. Standing all day long while Lady Muck swanned around issuing orders. I much prefer it here. I don't have to do much at all. Turn up and get the money each week. Suits me." She shrugged inelegantly. Barry thought that it probably did suit her down to the ground. He asked which of the two ladies behind the counter had also come from the Food Hall.

"Neither of them. Yolande left last month, went to new Smedleys' Soft Furnishings. Better money and more holidays. Lucky thing." It would seem that Sonia had been unable to stir herself sufficiently from her idle routine to find a better job. Barry dismissed the possibility of the potential poisoner being from Haberdashery and set off for Furnishings, his quarry a certain Mr Duke.

Unfortunately, Mr Duke was easily ruled out due to his marked tremor. The unlucky man had very shaky hands indeed. While neat writing was extremely difficult for him, he could easily manage larger motor activities such as the lifting and carrying required in the Furnishings Department. He was very co-operative and had such a pleasant manner that Barry quite warmed to him and ended up feeling very sorry for him. He could see how a move from the Food Hall was a welcome relief for Mr Duke and that he was glad to forget all about his time there.

Barry's next move was to interview young Mr Pearson in the Electrical Department. On being questioned, he shrugged off Barry's heavy-handed suggestion that he might feel sufficiently vindictive to mount an unspecified campaign against the Food Hall.

He beamed as he explained how happy he now was in Electricals.

"I just fit in here see?" he said "It's just the job for me. I can reach up to all the lamps and the high switches and let the others deal with the smaller appliances." He became positively enthusiastic discussing his new responsibilities and friendly colleagues. Barry discounted him. He very obviously wouldn't want anything to affect his employment at Murrays.

So, one had already left, one was too lazy to bother, one was too shaky to have written any sort of legible note and one was patently too happy at Murrays to endanger the store in any way. There was only one more person on the list. He set off down the stairs to the porters' office before checking his watch and, noting that lunch break was approaching, retracing his steps and continuing up to the canteen.

Jock was already seated at their usual table. He looked up and raised a hand in greeting. Barry went to the counter, closely supervised the overloading of a large plateful of mince and tatties, and then walked across to join him.

"How did you get on?" Jock queried.

"Not much luck with any of them so far. Just one left to grill," Barry responded through a mouthful.

"Which one?"

"The one now 'working' with the porters."

They both laughed. The porters were well known to be somewhat lacking in their understanding of a day's work. Their leader, Jim Hudson, was a keen but unsuccessful trade unionist forever declaring that staff must put down their tools in support of something or other. The other departments mostly ignored his demands but the men under his direct command had to adhere to his work ethic. This meant that all departments were in a permanent state of irritation at delays in deliveries that they knew had already arrived and were just awaiting transfer from the loading bay. That was if the loading bay was not already in use as a football pitch for the unofficial matches against porters from other stores and businesses around the area.

"Oh God," groaned Barry, "I can't say I relish tackling that lot. Trying to question one of Jim's boys could bring the whole department to a standstill."

Jock agreed, nodding silently. The two men

contemplated how best to tackle the porters' latest recruit without inflaming Jim to new heights of irritation against the management.

Jim was a small man with a large but constantly frustrated personality. He struggled to hold his head high in the presence of other shop stewards due to the Murrays managements' perceived intransigence. To his continued annoyance, Miss Murray insisted that Murrays be completely fair to their staff. Her time in large department stores in other capital cities had demonstrated the value of involving staff and giving them the incentive to work their hardest. She made sure this was in their interests: if Murrays had a good year, the percentage increase in profits was returned to the staff as a percentage pay rise. Very occasionally, a bonus would be declared. As she often stated, to Mr McElvey's despair, "Fair's fair. We must share the profits that they helped to earn us." Some years, of course, no profit was made or even a small loss was incurred, but no resultant reduction was made in staff pay. Thus, the staff appreciated the financial situation and also the consideration of their boss. This resulted in indifference to the calls for action, or rather inaction, by the shop steward.

"Could the letter be from Jim himself? Could it possibly be," ventured Barry, "an attempt to punish the management?"

"Surely not," replied Jock after some thought. "It's a funny thing to do, don't you think? It risks the whole shop. Anyway, there's no 'retrieval' aspect to it."

"What do you mean?" Barry looked searchingly at his friend.

"Well it just says 'you'd better find the poison in the food hall before a customer does.' It doesn't say, 'unless you give us another day off or a pay rise,' or anything. It doesn't look like there's anything in it for the writer, he or she doesn't offer any way out. It's not a ransom note." He lapsed and took a long draught of his orange-coloured tea.

"It could be a union thing though," persisted Barry, by this time certain the union was behind it. "I'll need to raise the possibility with the management." He really felt he was on to something.

Mrs Pegram grudgingly agreed that it could be a threat from the porters. She did support Jock's view, however, that there didn't seem to be more to it than a threat against the entire store. The risk of a customer being poisoned was insupportable. The Food Hall had been closed now for almost two days. Questions were being asked. The staff were unsettled and unhappy at having to deal with customers' enquiries about its closure. At the management meeting it was agreed to call Jim up to the boardroom to discuss the matter.

"He'll appreciate being involved." Mr Philipson felt. "Might cheer him up a bit, make him feel more important." Miss Murray nodded in agreement.

Mr McElvey snorted, his views on the trade

union leader were well known.

Fifteen minutes later, Jim blustered into the room.

"What's all this I hear?" he declared loudly, having jumped to all sorts of inaccurate conclusions on being summoned to the boardroom. "My boys at fault for the closure of the Food Hall?"

"Now, now," said Miss Murray kindly, albeit unwisely, as though addressing a child, "No one's blaming the porters."

Incensed at being patronised, Jim continued, "I've had enough of management's attitude to the workers here!"

Even more unwisely, Mr McElvey burst into loud laughter.

"What man? Had enough of a fair day's work for a fair day's pay?" he asked. "As if the porters do that!" he added as an afterthought, looking around at the others in expectation of agreement.

"Mr McElvey!" shouted Miss Murray and Mrs Pegram in irritated unison. Jim was never one to miss the chance to take offence and he grasped this golden opportunity with both hands. His eyes bulged and a vein throbbed in his throat.

"Well that's it." he whispered almost to himself, then: "All out!" he shouted hoarsely to no one in particular and turning on his heel he marched out of the room.

"Apologise at once!" said Mr Soames urgently, alas too late, as they observed Jim's departing brown-coated back. High dudgeon didn't exactly cover what it conveyed. He could be heard ranting all down the corridor towards the canteen.

The management team slumped back in their seats, casting despairing glances towards Mr McElvey.

"What have you done now?" Miss Murray hissed at him.

With airy indifference he stood up. "Well if there's nothing else to discuss I'll get back to work." He left the room stiffly. The others looked at each other.

"Brace yourselves." Miss Murray breathed as they all stood up and went thoughtfully back to their offices.

"What next?" Mrs Pegram wondered wearily.

Jim Hudson had marched straight to the staff canteen where second break was in full swing. The loud hubbub was punctuated by shrieks of laughter from the Cosmetics and Perfumery girls and bursts of coughing from the smokers' section. From his coat pocket Jim produced a whistle and gave three sharp blasts on it. Conversation faltered at all the tables around the room. From the kitchen, oblivious to the drama, Mrs Collins continued to tunelessly urge someone to, "Hit me with your rhythm stick." The juniors, at their table under the window, giggled nervously.

"Brothers and sisters," Jim began pompously, "Now is the time to withdraw your labour, the time to show your support for your beleaguered brothers, the time to show a united front to our enemy: the management!"

He took a deep breath ready for another oratorical outburst once he had worked out what to say.

Meanwhile, muttering was breaking out at every table as the staff quizzed each other on what was going on. Was the management our enemy wondered several of the more senior tables. Who exactly were the beleaguered brothers pondered Menswear. What would happen if their labour was withdrawn? Would they still get paid the juniors queried. Questions and worries echoed around the room. Whatever had happened it was certainly a serious matter. Jim was questioned closely about what had led to his momentous pronouncements. The staff were used to him trying to get them to strike over apparent trivialities, but this seemed a much graver situation. He explained in his loudest voice that the porters were being blamed for threatening to poison customers. This would inevitably lead to the closure of the store as, if word got out, customers would obviously boycott Murrays.

"– and who could blame them!" shouted one wag getting carried away.

A well-spoken voice called out in a cut-glass accent, "So was it you then? Was it the porters who wrote the poison pen letter?"

Jim hadn't spotted Miss McFarlane at a table in the corner with Miss Butters. Talk of a poison pen letter rippled through the room. Staff coming up for a late tea break stood in the doorway asking what was going on. The letter had not been common knowledge.

"Of course not!" gasped Jim with heavy emphasis. "As if we'd put everyone's livelihoods at risk!" He was appalled that people could think that. He was a sincere man who took his responsibilities as shop steward very seriously and, beyond that, he really cared about the welfare and security of his brothers and sisters in employment as he thought of them. Those next to him could see he was very upset and his anger was turning to despair. He was near to tears as conflicting emotions raged through his small frame. The room was silent.

"Fair enough. I believe you," said Mr Smith of Menswear. "What next then? Should we go to discuss this with the management? Perhaps Miss Murray herself?" he offered reasonably.

"No. Yes. I don't know. I think I'll need to speak to the Union about this. We'll need to do this properly if we're going to close down the store. I'll keep you all informed."

He called over his shoulder as he agitatedly moved towards one door then the other, eventually taking the door furthest from the management corridor and hurrying away to telephone the branch secretary from the porters' department extension.

"Close down the store!" rippled through the room. Some staff members were more aghast than others; the juniors relished the excitement. Older employees shook their heads, unsure if they had actually agreed to anything in the way of industrial action.

Mrs Carr, the management secretary, had been poised outside the door to listen to what was going on. She quickly turned, re-entered the management corridor and sought out Miss Murray. She found her deep in conversation with Mrs Pegram in her office. Without hesitating, she walked in, "They're going to strike Miss Murray. That porter says he's going to close down the shop."

"Oh God. Surely not. He just misunderstood what was being said," sighed Miss Murray.

"Well maybe not," put in Mrs Pegram, "After all, we were acting on Barry's suggestion, and it was only a suggestion, that the porters might have written that note."

"True enough," nodded Miss Murray, "but we can't have him calling out all the staff. How was it going down with them Mrs Carr?" she questioned, frowning anxiously.

"Quite well I'd say. Nobody actually disagreed. They seemed quite concerned about a department being thought to have put the whole store at risk."

"Even though that's exactly what a strike would, itself do. Oh God," Miss Murray repeated in dismay.

As the three women were pondering what to do, Miss Murray tapping the table top restlessly, Mrs Pegram pacing and Mrs Carr wringing her hands, there was a timid knock at the door. Mrs Carr looked questioningly at Miss Murray who nodded, and she went to open it. To their surprise Miss Butters sidled in, doing a slight double take at finding Miss Murray herself there.

"I wis jist wanting a wee word with Mrs Pegram," she announced hoarsely.

"I'm afraid we're a bit busy just now," Mrs Pegram responded.

"Could you come back in the morning do you think?" she enquired pleasantly.

"If the shop's open in the morning." Miss Murray cut in gloomily with a big sigh.

"That's it though. That's whit I was wanting to talk aboot," the dishevelled little woman persisted.

"You'd better come in then Miss Butters."

"Aye well I jist wanted to see you Mrs Pegram, no that one," her chin dipped respectfully as she indicated Miss Murray. She seemed afraid to even look at her directly.

"There's nothing you can't say in front of Miss Murray," Mrs Pegram said kindly, "but Mrs Carr I wonder if you could excuse us? Thank you." With noticeably bad grace, Mrs Carr left the room, closing the door sharply behind her.

"Now what seems to be the matter?" opened Miss Murray kindly, taking pity on the shy little woman in front of her. "Perhaps we should all sit down?"

She indicated a chair for Miss Butters.

They sat down and Mrs Pegram and Miss Murray looked expectantly at her as she began.

"It's like this," she started. "To let you

understand...." she faltered, then in a burst, "It wis me." She glared suddenly up at the two startled women.

"You what?" asked Mrs Pegram.

"Ah did it. Ah wrote thon letter."

"You wrote the letter about there being poison in the Food Hall?"

"Aye."

"But why? Why would you do such a thing? You've worked there for years. I thought you liked it?"

"Aye I do." She looked momentarily downcast. "I did," she continued defiantly, looking up suddenly. Seeing the incomprehension written all over Miss Murray and Mrs Pegram's faces, she continued, "I've had enough you see. I cannae stand seeing that woman treating people the way she does. She's poison, she's the poison herself."

"You mean there are no actual poisoned goods in the Food Hall?" Miss Murray asked slowly.

"No. Just her."

Rapidly summing up the situation, Mrs Pegram asked, "So you're saying there's no risk to our customers at all? And no risk to the store's reputation?"

"No just the staff. But she cannae go on like that. She cannae go on being cruel to poor souls like my laddie." The outburst continued with increased vehemence.

Mrs Pegram pricked up her ears, "Your laddie, er boy?"

"Aye, Darren Smith. He's my laddie. I had him when I was that young. My mother said I couldnae keep him but my sister did. She's married," she added with a defiant nod.

Daylight was dawning for Miss Murray. "We must speak to Jim Hudson at once. We must completely exonerate the porters and put a stop to this strike." She had a thought. "Does Miss McFarlane know?"

"Of course not," scoffed Miss Butters. She was well aware that there was no longer any possibility of her continued employment at Murrays and she had nothing further to lose.

A notice went up in the canteen:

> The management team wish to make it quite clear that the Porters' Department played no part in the recent closure of the Food Hall and to apologise for any distress that their actions in this regard may have inadvertently caused.

Naturally, there was a very difficult interview between Jim Hudson and the management team. Various concessions had to be made and the porters now rejoiced in an extra fifteen-minute break each day and an extra week's holiday a year. Mr McElvey almost had to take a day off to recover from the negotiations. The Food Hall reopened and did a roaring trade under its new manager, Alan from the third-floor Tea Room. He had been due for promotion and it was felt that his people skills would be an asset as the department recovered from its years under Miss McFarlane's iron rule. Miss Butters, as she had suspected, became surplus to requirements and found herself another job in a local grocer's shop where she unnerved the customers with her dark comments about her previous employers and general muttering.

Miss McFarlane was a different matter. Redeploying her was not straightforward. As she saw it, she had done nothing wrong, she had only sought to do her best for her employers. Mrs Pegram thought about it. Given that she was a proven hard worker with high standards but less in the way of people skills, it was thought that she might be best placed where there were extra hours to fill. The porters, to allow for their extended breaks and longer holidays, would need to have their numbers increased.

Surely Miss McFarlane could be useful; she could be counted on to efficiently tally up the paperwork on the arrival of goods, organising timeous deliveries to each department.

"Perfect," said Miss Murray when she heard about the plan.

"All out!" said Jim (but not aloud – yet).

Chapter 14

The Biter Bit

"The trouble with Neville is that people just don't like him," his mother confided to her sister over coffee in Murrays' Tea Room. She reflected for a moment, "In fact, I don't like him very much." She eyed her sister anxiously as she expressed this long held, long repressed opinion.

Her sister desperately tried to think of something reassuring to say but could think of nothing more consoling than to pat her hand nervously and ask if she'd like another scone. Privately, she was, of course, in entire agreement with her unfortunate sister and had held the same view since Neville was an irritable baby, awkward toddler, horrible child, deeply unpleasant youth, and had continued his career in unpopularity into his twenties.

It was not that he wasn't clever. He was. Extremely so. However, this intelligence took a most disagreeable form: he thoroughly enjoyed finding out other people's secrets. Not just any secrets either. He revelled in making discoveries of a negative nature and, where possible, broadcasting them to the maximum discomfort of his unfortunate victim. He was extremely skilled at this. His talent in the field manifested itself at an early age. As a six-year-old guest at a classmate's party (invited in the interests of fairness against the birthday boy's wishes, "Oh, Mum. Not Neville!"), his exhaustive searches

214

through the bathroom cabinet revealed all sorts of embarrassing truths. He found that the kindly and hitherto glamorous hostess dyed her hair, that the presence of anti-haemorrhoid preparations underpinned her husband's general snappiness, and that the birthday boy had very recently suffered from nits. All of this was relayed to an interested audience of children and their parents seated in expectation of the magician's appearance.

His appalled mother led him instantly away. His protests, "But it's true Mum, the bottle said 'Glorious Blonde' on it!" echoed through the hall and could be heard in the street even after the stony-faced hostess slammed the front door after them.

So it had continued. He was soon in trouble at school, Boy Scouts and even at Sunday school where he related his discovery of the minister's secret supply of gin to all and sundry one memorable Sunday morning. His mother could no longer attend that particular place of worship thereafter. Discussing the results of their only son's latest sleuthing was often looked on by his mother as the last straw for her husband. He had sighed and shaken his head, then slowly closed his eyes and sunk into a lethargy from which he never recovered. Of course, Neville was keen to inform his classmates of his father's suicide attempt with an overdose of antidepressants.

Neville enjoyed his visits to the psychiatric hospital where his father now lived and found many opportunities to read through the other patients' medical notes and pass on the most interesting of his discoveries to their, generally horrified, visitors. Various members of the staff were duly censured and one negligent nurse found her employment at an end after certain of Neville's lurid revelations. Neville felt he had found his niche as an investigator at a very early age.

It is sometimes the case that the most reprehensible of people have the nicest friends, or at least one. So it was with Neville. Peter Gibson had been Neville's firm friend since nursery school (despite having been exposed by Neville to his classmates as not being entirely reliable as to his toilet training and therefore occasionally suffering accidents to a greater or lesser extent). The nursery staff couldn't fathom Peter's attachment to young Neville, yet he remained loyal to his nasty friend. This friendship continued throughout his school career where, naturally, Neville shone briefly as editor of the school magazine until his exposé of the gym master's punishment exercises. Having been relieved of his editorial role, Neville threw himself into his studies, determined to follow his ideal career as an investigative journalist. The Headmaster couldn't deny that this could, indeed, be a way forward for the least popular pupil he'd ever had. He was only sorry that Peter seemed to be drawn sufficiently into Neville's ambit to want to follow the same career path. The view from the staff room was that Peter was destined for a caring profession. However, it was not to be and the two young men moved on to college to study journalism.

Here Neville shone. The lecturers, mostly retired journalists burnt out after a lifetime of news gathering and snooping, were thrilled with their new recruit. Neville was adept at sniffing out secrets and relating them, to the discomfort of others. He had a great turn of phrase and memorable examples of this included 'Police Parking Predicament' (when an officious policeman accidentally arranged for a royal duchess's car to be towed away while on a visit to the college), 'Carry out Carry on' (after a fracas in the canteen), and 'College Principal Doesn't Give a Flying Faux Pas at Funeral' (when the Principal erroneously credited a deceased staff member with a British Empire Medal rather than his Distinguished Flying Cross. Family members were reported to be 'appalled').

Peter developed something of a reputation for himself as an apologist for his reptilian friend. His friendly, open face and kindly intonation as he sympathised with Neville's victims did much to amend some potentially difficult situations. He developed his skills in writing responses for the college magazine's agony column and fabricated the horoscopes with disarming ease. According to these, life was to be a bowl of cherries in one way or another for everyone. Everyone felt the better for reading Peter's pages. They helped the reader to recover from the shocks of reading Neville's latest front page revelation.

Peter had become a rather handsome young man

and the journalism staff felt that he could have a career in television or film rather than print media. He was not unwilling to try this and, unsurprisingly, he came over well on screen; he looked good and his pleasing voice transmitted his sympathetic personality. To Neville's dismay, it looked as though his friend might surpass him as star of their course. Peter, loyalty personified, reassured him, "I'd be nothing without your stories to talk about on screen," he told him. "I need you to keep sleuthing and turning up stories for me."

Neville accepted this and a two-way alliance was formed. Peter was front man and Neville did all the dirty work.

This proved very lucrative for the duo. After a period of employment, first in local radio, then regional TV, the two of them struck out as independent producers. Their documentaries were a great hit with the public and the TV companies fell over themselves trying to buy up their latest scandal-strewn production. A pharmaceutical company folded and very serious questions were asked after an in-depth documentary on a local army regiment was aired to a horrified public.

Sitting in their office one day, Neville looked at Peter. "You know, we're on to something here," he breezed. "Where there's muck there's brass." Peter nodded and Neville continued, "Where to next though? There's something about institutions, large companies that seem useful to think about."

Peter agreed. "Yes, if there are lots of people,

some better off than others, lots of opportunity for petty crime and so on, there's more chance of a story or even several."

He continued, warming to his theme. "We can't get into hospitals without all sorts of permissions we'd never get, we've done the army – or done for it," he laughed. "What does that leave? The Scouts?"

"Nah, too obvious," continued Neville. "Something commercial rather than voluntary is what we need," he mused. "A big business, say, or even, I know… a shop." He looked at Peter with eyebrows raised.

"I see where you're coming from," agreed Peter. "A big shop. Do you mean something like one of the chain stores? That would be a slog up and down the country. Massive expenses to outlay first."

"No, something more local, home grown. Something like…" he paused. "How about Murrays?"

"Murrays, now that's an idea," Peter nodded slowly.

Four weeks later the two men sat in the boardroom waiting for the management team to arrive. "Remember, leave the talking to me," urged Peter, peering anxiously at his friend.

"Okay, okay, I get it," Neville replied, holding his hands up in mock surrender. At that moment the door opened and Mrs Carr edged in with a loaded coffee tray. Peter rushed to help. "What a nice young man," she thought and smiled at him. The others filed into the room and sat down, looking questioningly at Peter and Neville.

Miss Murray called the meeting to order and introduced the two visitors.

"These are the people who want to make a documentary about us," she started. "They are interested in the old department stores and want to highlight their relevance to modern day shoppers." She looked at Neville. "That's right isn't it? I think that's what you said."

Peter interrupted before Neville could answer her.

"Exactly right Miss Murray. We feel that Murrays has such a lot to demonstrate to shoppers and even, believe it or not, to the newer chain stores. Murrays' customer service is streets ahead of other shops and you have such interesting stock."

Mr McElvey looked up from his notes for the first time. Sensing an opportunity for free advertising on prime-time television, he cut in enthusiastically.

"Of course. We do things differently and better. There's a slogan for you." He looked triumphantly round at the others. No one could call him out of touch.

"Lovely Mr, er, McElvey is it?" Peter responded. "You have a gift for apt advertising phrases! I assume you work in that side of the business?" He feigned amazement when he was assured that Mr McElvey only worked in Accounts. "What a nice young man," Mr McElvey thought.

The smiles continued around the table as they were each assured that the documentary crew would in no way impinge on business and was, indeed, highly likely to lead to an increase in customers. It was decided to give the go ahead to the project.

"That's one in the eye to our competition!" Mr Soames proclaimed before explaining to Neville and Peter that they had deadly rivals in the retail industry.

"Indeed," said Neville, smiling weakly but, as usual, sensing a nasty opportunity.

Neville and Peter, as the company partners, didn't do all the dirty work themselves. For this they recruited young, enthusiastic researchers keen to gain a toehold in the world of film and television documentary making and pleasingly happy to accept very little remuneration. For the 'Murrays project,' as they called it, they used three young people straight out of university. Carrie, William and Theo did their best to ingratiate themselves with the senior partners. Each was keener than the last to come up with angles and potential stories for the project. They were well trained in what they needed to do: the technical, social, psychological and strictly practical aspects of their jobs.

At the initial briefing meeting, after the almost obligatory ice breaking and introductory exercises had been carried out in a perfunctory way, Neville got down to explaining what was wanted: "We need you to ferret out potential storylines. We're looking for dissatisfied customers, underhand behaviour, overcharging, unhappy junior staff, bullying, poor terms and conditions at work, all the usual sorts of thing."

Carrie blinked. It wasn't what she'd expected. She'd thought they would be trying to identify key staff members and customers to interview as well as checking out the technical side of things. She looked at William who, she knew, had a background in camera work. Maybe they'd get him to do that side of things? But no, Neville continued to outline the unpleasant angles he was looking for. Gosh, she thought, he's really looking for trouble. This didn't look as if it was going to be the enjoyable assignment she'd hoped for.

Theo wanted to know in more detail exactly what was required. He sketched out a proforma on a notepad and showed it to Neville and Peter.

"Yes, that's pretty much what's wanted," confirmed Peter with a smile. "Share that with the others will you. It looks a good way to summarise your impressions and it'll certainly speed up our meetings." He stood up. "Right then. We'll meet up here in the boardroom at 5pm each evening to compare notes and make more specific plans prior to filming." The others nodded and collected up their papers. Theo arranged to share copies of his proforma.

The next day each of the researchers set to work. They started in different departments throughout the store and tried hard to ingratiate themselves with the staff while smiling pleasantly at any customers who looked enquiringly at them. They had been equipped with business cards to give out explaining who they were if anyone asked.

Researcher Report No1

Researcher: Carrie
Dept.: China and Glass
Number of staff: 6
Senior staff: 2
Junior staff: 4

<u>Dept. description</u>: large, open area, island display units (various) wall units, sales desks (2) rear packing area. NOTE: Lighting not good. Filming would require special lighting to be set up.

<u>Storylines</u>: dead end? Highly satisfied customers (5 willing to be filmed. Details taken). Stock conspicuously of high quality and department well maintained. Staff atmosphere and morale noticeably good – all staff willing to be filmed.

<u>Query</u>: not for us?

Researcher Report No2
Researcher: William
Dept.: Security
Staff: 1 head of dept.
Three part-time day staff (store detectives)
Three part-time night staff (security guards)
1 dog (night time only) small

Dept. description: small office for manager, lockers for staff. All wear own clothes.

Storylines: manager very voluble. Keen to be filmed. Highly satisfied with performance of his dept. Day staff quiet but no complaints about any aspect of their employment. Not much interaction between them as they all work on an individual basis. Unobtrusive filming unlikely to be possible due to undercover nature of the work.

Query: not for us? Nothing much of note. Not as interesting as we thought it would be, although head of department thinks it is.

<u>Researcher Report No3</u>
Researcher: Theo
Dept.: Porters
Staff: 2 seniors (?) hard to say who the boss is
4 general porters
1 part-time night porter as required

<u>Storylines</u>: odd atmosphere? Armed neutrality? 2 at same level. Civil but others work away. No complaints. Scared to? Pay and conditions seem to be better than other shop staff. Worth investigating? Not very interesting to film though.

Peter and Neville had been staying with Neville's mother while working on the Murrays project.

Neville explained to Peter, "I like to stay with the old girl from time to time. Keep an eye on my inheritance!"

Peter gasped. He thought he was used to the way Neville's mind worked, but sometimes, like now, he was taken aback. He didn't reply.

Neville's mother took great pleasure looking after the two boys, as she still thought of them, and laid on huge suppers for them after their days at Murrays. After the meal was cleared away she would sit with them at the dining room table listening in on their discussions and plans. She had always been a rather shy and self-effacing woman and was far too inhibited to try to join in the conversation. It felt to her like an honour to be allowed to listen in on the famous documentary makers. Neville and Peter hardly noticed her except when she tried to press them to have another cup of coffee or more biscuits.

"Not now, Mother," Neville snapped. She subsided quietly back into her chair.

The two men looked at the researchers' papers. They were very disappointing. Neville was angry and presumed there was some problem with the researchers themselves rather than their findings.

"They're too mousey," he raged. "They don't have the nerve to really push things. We need dirt not this stuff." He indicated the reports with a contemptuous hand. "There's nothing for it. I'll have to get going myself. I'd rather have kept out of the direct fact finding but needs must. This could be a big earner for us." A national TV channel had expressed interest in the project and was awaiting updates.

The next day, Neville set out around the store with a notebook and small sound recorder. He worked his way steadily from department to department. But somehow, he didn't seem to have a way with people. He couldn't seem to encourage staff or customers to unburden themselves to him. He sat fuming after dinner that evening.

"Nothing. Nothing. Nothing. What's wrong with this place? There must be something wrong somewhere."

Peter thought for a while. "Maybe it actually *is* OK? Maybe the staff just *are* pleasant and helpful and the customers just *like* the place?"

"Don't be ridiculous," came the smart rejoinder.

"Nowhere's perfect. We'll need to keep trying. You'll need to keep trying. It's your turn now." His mother opened her mouth to say something, but Neville snapped, "Keep out of it Mother. Stick to things you do know something about." She stood up stiffly and left the room. Peter looked at him reproachfully.

"That was a bit unnecessary."

"Who cares? We've got work to do. We've got to make this thing work."

"How about we take another angle? Do something completely different?" said Peter.

"Like what?"

"Well, how about an initially more positive, innovative angle."

"Yeeees, go on…"

"How about we do something wild like a live focus group? We could do it right in the heart of the shop? The camera angles and lighting would be so interesting, we could zoom in and out on people's faces…"

Neville, excited now, cut in, "And ask really pointed questions, get the sorts of dirt we need on live television. It could be the event of the year. Something really different. Yes, yes, yes. We'll do it!"

He had seldom been so enthused by a project. This would really sink Murrays.

The management team were keen for updates on what the researchers were finding and how the project was shaping up. Peter, sensing their ill-fated enthusiasm for the project, had no trouble in selling the idea for the live televised focus group as the heart of the programme. The idea was that various departments would be filmed and recorded in advance and shown before and after the live part of the programme. This would lead to a certain amount of upheaval of course: the Grand Hall would have to be cleared as it would be the most iconic location as Peter put it. This would also allow for the equipment to be set up as unobtrusively as possible around the galleries.

"Should we shut the shop for the day?" enquired Mr Soames to Mr McElvey's acute shock. Fortunately, it was decided that there would be no need for the curtailment of commercial activity.

"It might even be an attraction for the public," cut in Mr Richardson in excitement. Neville smiled grimly to himself as Peter nodded happily.

It was decided that Peter himself would act as question master to be briefed, via a headset, by Neville located just out of sight behind a bank of monitors behind a pillar in Menswear.

Later that week a group of rather self-conscious ladies found their seats in the semi-circle arranged around a small raised platform on which Peter was to sit as question master, or referee, as he jokingly put it to them. The Grand Hall had, as planned, been cleared and lighting and cameras were fixed on the galleries and focused down on the assembly. The chosen ladies had obviously dressed for the occasion and smart outfits, best coats and jackets and significant amounts of costume jewellery were much in evidence. Theo, Carrie and William had recruited them and briefed them on what would be expected. They were all very excited and apprehensive as they looked up at the cameras, bright lighting and suspended microphones ready to pick up their least utterance.

Looking on via a monitor in what was now referred to as the production area, Neville was surprised to see his mother seated near the centre of the group. He laughed to himself. Trust the old girl. Well, why not? She was a long-term customer after all. He spoke into his microphone connected to Peter's earpiece.

"Right. Get started." He signalled the cameras to action and quiet was called all around the store. The various technicians crouched to their duties.

Peter started by thanking them all for attending and explaining that the purpose of the group was to highlight their concerns about the store. The ladies looked puzzled. One, a staff member, requested clarification. Peter reiterated that in an enterprise such as this it was highly likely that, as he put it, the little people tended to lose out in the interests of profit making. Brows furrowed. It was after all a shop. It was in business to make money.

Another staff member started bravely, "Of course everyone could complain about pay but the conditions here are so…"

Peter interrupted interestedly, "Tell us more

about the poor pay?"

The flustered woman said, "That wasn't my point." She lapsed into embarrassed silence, unwilling to volunteer anything else to what now appeared to be a hostile interrogator. She looked around her. The others in the group were looking unhappy too.

Neville shouted into his microphone, "Keep going. For God's sake, keep going."

Peter looked around helplessly. "Any customers here like to tell us about their experiences at Murrays?"

This more positive line of questioning opened up floodgates of stories of kind staff operating above and beyond the call of duty, the painstaking sourcing of tiny, relatively inexpensive items, of shared jokes and friendly decade-long relationships between customers and individual members of staff. Neville could be heard virtually tearing his hair in the production area.

"No, no, no! Not this stuff!" He shouted unpleasant question after unpleasant question in Peter's earpiece. Peter manfully tried to comply but to little avail.

Eventually, Neville barked, "Shoplifting. Get them to tell us how much gets nicked. How the cost of this is passed on to customers, that sort of thing?"

Peter started to ask about this when he was interrupted by a quiet voice.

"Shoplifting. That's a nicer way of talking about stealing. It's theft really. No more and no less. My son's a shoplifter. A thief. Every year since he was a little boy he's stolen something from here for my birthday. And Christmas presents. I know he has. He told me. He's proud of it. Of getting something over on the shop. It's not very nice really. Not nice at all. He's not nice at all and now he's stealing again. He's trying to take Murrays' good name and it *is* a good name. They treat their staff fairly and the customers like coming here."

There was a thin cheer from the staff of Ladies Separates and Model Gowns hanging over the gallery rails.

She continued, her voice growing in confidence, "He's the one making this documentary. Peter here is just the front man. Neville's somewhere around making the bullets for Peter to fire. I'm ashamed of him. I'm ashamed of my own son. I'm ashamed of myself for staying quiet about it for so long."

She sat back down, her cheeks flaming; she was clearly on the point of tears. There was a stunned silence. Ladies in neighbouring seats reached over to pat her reassuringly. They all glared at Peter who sat still, for once flummoxed. There was silence in his ear. Neville had gone.

Later that day in the boardroom, Peter faced the angry management team.

"So," raged Mr McElvey, "What you intended all along was to make a scurrilous programme about us?"

"I'd prefer to say frank and open

documentary…" Peter faltered.

"Frank and open indeed," Miss Murray took up the baton. "You have wasted a great deal of our time in your attempt to misrepresent us and cause distress to our staff and customers. In fact, I'm not sure if there isn't a case to be made against you for loss of business at the very least. I feel sure that we could sue you for all you're worth."

She paused. "If you're actually worth anything at all," she added derisively.

"My colleague…" began Peter again.

"Yes? Do you mean the one we now know is a long-term shoplifter?"

"Yes. I mean…" Peter was floundering. He cursed Neville for landing him in this awkward situation. He didn't know what to say. Looking round the table at the angry faces he quailed. He had been warned so often about his association with Neville. Was this it then? The end of their friendship? He decided that it was. He stood up.

"I'm sorry. I'm so sorry. I don't know how I can make this up to you…"

"No. Neither do I." Miss Murray was uncharacteristically unrelenting. "We work hard to make this business as good as it can be and to be fair to our employees. Then someone like you comes along with the clear aim of undermining it all. Undermining us all…" She shook with barely suppressed rage. Fearing that her friend might actually hit the cowering young man, Mrs Pegram stood up and smoothly took over the situation.

"Right, well, you've done quite enough young man. I don't think there's anything more to be said. Now will you please remove yourself and all your equipment and staff immediately."

She ushered him to the door past the figure of Barry, standing there bristling with antagonism, clearly keen to take the young man outside and giving him a serious 'sort out' in the car park. He snarled menacingly.

"That's enough Barry." Mrs Pegram put paid to his hopes.

As Peter slunk out, Mr McElvey's voice called after him, "Don't think this is the end of it. You may well be hearing from our lawyers."

And Neville? After his precipitous departure from the shop he had walked the streets for some hours. Surely he had suffered the ultimate humiliation. To be so publicly denounced by his own mother. What could be worse? He ruminated on her. Stupid cow was his first thought. Then his mind moved on in its usual nasty way to how to pay her back. But just where he expected to find a solution he found a strange blank. He couldn't think how to do it. There wasn't anything left to do to hurt her that he hadn't already done at one time or another in his life. That thought brought him to a standstill. Passers-by stared at the white-faced young man as he held his hands to his face and groaned. He had lied and cheated and embarrassed his mother time and again, and, by his reprehensible behaviour, led her to be isolated from her church and her friends. He had taken advantage of his own father's weak mental state. He thought further. He was the absolute personification of a bad son. The best thing he could do would be to remove himself from her life. And Peter's. Somewhere within him, he dimly perceived that he had not been a good friend to Peter. He had left him spluttering at the cameras and a row of outraged ladies, trying to somehow restore order to the situation after his mother's outburst. He'd even left him to carry the can with the Murrays management. He had got him into this trouble, this career even. He realised now that he'd lost him. He'd lost his best friend. He'd lost everything. If only they hadn't gone to Murrays.

He'd come away from that store once again with something he hadn't paid for in a financial sense anyway – a conscience at last. It hurt.

Chapter 15

Chameleon/Chimera

Mrs Pegram looked at the vision of loveliness standing in front of her dressed in the smartest of haute couture casual wear. She marvelled at the fine features and the beautiful black hair that cascaded in a sparkle of curls from a central parting.

Wow, she thought, what a stunner! She smiled as she responded to his initial greeting.

"How lovely to meet you at last, Antoine. We were expecting you last week. Miss Murray has told me so much about your father and the store in Paris."

His voice when he spoke was an aural evocation of his appearance – just as gorgeous. He purred in a deep voice and a thrilling French accent.

"The pleasure is all mine Meeses Pegram." He looked deeply into her eyes as he said this. She found herself quite flushed and embarrassed at her own reaction. Crossly, she told herself to get a grip.

She went on, "Now Antoine, you don't mind if I call you Antoine?"

"Ah, non," he reassured her. "Everyone calls me Antoine." He flashed her another of his devastating smiles.

"Miss Murray has told me about how she came to work in your father's company as part of her training. I assume this is some sort of delayed reciprocal arrangement?"

235

"Well, yes I hope so. My father told me so much about Miss Murray and her shop. I want to find out how the British shopper shops so I can sell more to them when I return to Paris," he explained.

"Well I'm not sure exactly how much you can learn about that here but we can try to help. Is there a particular department you want to spend time in or do you want to shadow one of the management perhaps?"

"Non. Not the management." He stifled her hopes of prolonged exposure to his charm. "Perhaps a little time in as many departments as possible?"

"Right," she pondered the most useful starting point for him. "Is there a particular focus for your store in Paris?" she queried. "I mean do you mostly cover fashion or cosmetics or household goods for example?"

"Household goods?" He shuddered. "Oh no. We supply ladies, not their staff. We have the best designer clothes, hats and jewellery for the smartest dressers in Paris."

She stifled a gasp at his blatant snobbery. When or if she got to know him better she'd tell him not to say such things out loud. He was welcome to think them of course.

Antoine's first day in Model Gowns went well. Mrs Hope was slightly taken aback at his super smart, beautifully-cut business suit, exquisite tie and long, carefully coiffed hair. He breezed into the department exuding a very slight scent of exclusive cologne. "How lovely," she thought. Then, "What a sweetie, must be gay." The others in the department and the adjoining Ladies Wear Department all came to the same conclusion. He was clearly very knowledgeable about cutting-edge fashion and, if Murrays' stock seemed rather less than 'a la mode,' he was tactful enough not to say it out loud.

Thanks to his cutting but absolutely correct remarks on his customers' appearances, up till now Mr da Costa had been the main attraction of Model Gowns. He was unsure about this wonderful new addition to the staff, taken aback at finding someone with the same fashion skills as himself, but a much more tactful way of putting it to the ladies. Direct as ever, he asked, "Who are you anyway? Why are you here?"

Mrs Hope was secretly surprised that he didn't go the whole hog and ask, "Who do you think you are?" However, he refrained from that level of directness. Mr da Costa wasn't an aggressive person.

Antoine handled the potentially difficult conversation with admirable aplomb and smoothness. In his quiet, sincere voice, he responded. "I hope to learn from you all here in Scotland. Where I live, the ladies care more for style than comfort. This shows in their faces I think. They can have a strained look. Your ladies here have radiant complexions and relaxed faces. This takes years off them, I feel. I want to learn how to do this for my ladies back home."

Mr da Costa nodded, both relieved and

convinced. Listening female members of staff reached up to their faces as though to check for this hitherto unsuspected beneficial side effect of their elasticated waistbands and comfortable shoes. They nodded in satisfaction, impressed at his discernment.

He remained in Model Gowns for several weeks, just enough time for him to gather respect and admiration from staff and even some customers. Mr da Costa was slightly disconcerted to find that one of his key clients, Margo Clapperton, had been into the department during one of his breaks and had not waited for him. Antoine had overcome her objections to his selection of clothing and she had been delighted to purchase a whole range of cruise wear. Mr da Costa had previously been informed of this forthcoming cruise and prepared a selection of items for her. It was fortunate that Antoine had concurred on this and basically sold her the clothes Mr da Costa had already put aside for her. She was delighted with the outfits and even more delighted to be served by such a polite and respectful young man.

"Quite a contrast." She told the 'girls' at the golf club. "I usually need to brace myself before going to Model Gowns. You just don't know what Mr D will say next!" The 'girls' took note.

Mr da Costa mused on Antoine's way with his ladies and practised Antoine's interested gaze and knowing nod as one customer after another blurted out her hopes and fears for her next social engagement. He found that he didn't actually need to say much at all, but instead he should leave the lady concerned to think that she, herself, had selected the perfect outfit for the event in question.

Antoine's time in Model Gowns was thus a tremendous success. He moved onto the next department with good luck messages ringing in his ears.

Antoine had requested that he be placed in as wide a variety of departments as possible. To Mrs Pegram's surprise, he had asked to be assigned to the porters next.

"But why?" she asked him. "I thought you were mostly interested in the sales aspect of the shop."

"Ah Meeses Pegram, but they are integral to the smooth working of it all." He waved his arms gracefully to indicate the whole store. "They convey the stock to all the departments, they are the arteries of the store and keep it all going. Without them, phut! Every department would grind to a halt. I want to find out where the blockages are, and the 'aneurisms', where the arterial bleeds occur, where the cholesterol builds up in the system."

An odd metaphor, thought Mrs Pegram, but she saw his point. "Very well. I'll have a word with Jim our head porter and you can start there on Monday.

She looked up at him pointedly. "I should say that they start at 7.30am, not 9am like the others."

He waved away this information. "I will be there."

"Dressed appropriately too," she added with a

lingering look at his exquisite suit.

"Mais oui!" With an elegant wave he left the office and wandered off down the customers' carpeted staircase.

The following Monday, a grumbling Jim unlocked the door to the porters' lodge, as their subterranean department was called. He sat down on an upturned crate and shouted to Darren, the newest member of the team, to bring him a cup of tea.

"And mind you make it strong enough," he added. He had been most annoyed to hear from Mrs Pegram that they were to be joined by some French bloke coming to learn from them. "Look for trouble more like." He had told her, concluding suspiciously, "I hope this isn't some sort of management spy. I'll not have it!"

"Just wait and see," Mrs Pegram reassured him. "I'm sure you'll find him, er, interesting."

As Jim gulped down the dregs of his tea, he became aware of a slight commotion outside. The door was pushed open and a tall young man entered. His hair was tied back and roughly secured in a knot at the back; he was wearing tattered jeans and the sleeves of an old checked shirt were pushed up above his elbows revealing lurid tattoos on both forearms.

"You Jim?" he enquired rudely. "I'm Mac."

"Mac?" queried Jim. "I'm expecting a French bloke."

"Antoine – Tony – Tony Macaroni – Mac. OK with you? Now where do I start?"

"Right," Jim answered weakly. "Let me see now. Darren," he shouted. "Bring me the deliveries schedule. God knows where that McFarlane woman has put it." (The McFarlane woman was on holiday – to everyone's relief.)

'Mac' turned out to be a great success with the porters. He was extremely knowledgeable about the important things in life: football and beer. He played football very well and was promoted to the store's first team for the annual needle match between Murrays and their rival store. He didn't score the winning goal, but set it up beautifully for one of the others. The celebrations went on long into the night. He proved not to be just a man's man either. The sight of his strapping figure pushing the large trolley of deliveries round the store led to many a frisson among the female staff around the galleries. The canteen was fizzing with chat about the new pin-up in the Porters' Department.

Beyond his football and his magnetic attraction to women, Mac was also a useful addition to the Porters' Department. He identified some key issues and made practical suggestions for addressing them. The unwieldy trolleys loaded up with stock from the basement store rooms were extremely heavy and awkward to manoeuvre. This was invariably a two-man job. In addition, it wasn't always possible to steer them to the departmental stock rooms, necessitating their unloading onto the shop floor and the transferring of the boxes by hand by the shop assistants. This was untidy and inefficient. Mac sourced a supply of smaller, more easily manoeuvred trolleys that could be managed by one man and could transport goods directly to the departmental stock rooms. No mess and no extra work for shop floor staff. Everyone agreed that they were an excellent innovation. Even Mr McElvey seemed happy enough to sign off their cost.

Mac left the Porter's Department after another few weeks following a huge departmental farewell night out involving the consumption of industrial quantities of alcohol and the singing of many sentimental songs. He agreed that he was not indeed "awa tae bide awa" and presented himself with a remarkably clear head the next day in Mrs Pegram's office.

Where to next, she wondered. He had gone down so well in such disparate departments that it was hard to believe he was the same man. She looked at him smiling blandly at her, all traces of Mac erased.

"The main restaurant perhaps?" she suggested. "I don't know if you're interested in the catering side of things?"

"Ah oui, what an interesting idea," he breathed smiling intently at her and leaning forward. She was irritated to find herself blushing again. She was far too old for that sort of thing she told herself angrily. "Right then. I'll speak to the head chef and will let you know what he says. In the meantime, why not have a few days off? You're staying with Miss Murray at Rosehill, aren't you?"

"Oh yes. I'm being quite spoilt by Mrs Glen and the girls. They know how to look after me."

Mrs Pegram was uncertain whether the redoubtable Mrs Glen would be likely to fall victim to his roguish charm. However, it sounded like she had. She dismissed him and resolved to discuss him with Miss Murray.

At coffee that morning the two women talked about their French intern.

"He's done so well both in Model Gowns and with the Porters," Mrs Pegram informed her friend. "He seems to charm everyone. How's he doing at home? Has Mrs Glen fallen at his feet?"

"Well, no, not quite, but he is easily her favourite ever house guest." In answer to Mrs Pegram's enquiring expression, Miss Murray continued, "He keeps his room immaculately tidy, you'd hardly believe he slept in the bed or used the bathroom at all. He does his own washing and prefers to cook for himself. Quite remarkable in a man!" The two nodded thoughtfully and the conversation moved on.

The head chef in Murrays' Restaurant was a Mr Pargeter. A very serious and hardworking man, he'd been employed in Murrays' kitchens since he was first apprenticed there and had worked his way up over the years to head chef. A man of few words, most of them spoken in a vaguely menacing hiss, he knew exactly what diners expected in Murrays' Restaurant.

In response to a restaurant critic complaining of the formulaic nature of the menu, he had snapped, "Of course it's formulaic. I know the formula for what keeps Murrays' diners coming back." The management team could only concur. The Restaurant remained popular with their customers who seemed to prefer the certainty of the old favourite dishes to any new fancy menu items. When informed of Antoine's placement in the kitchen he had shrugged. A new person was neither here nor there to Mr Pargeter. He would soon enough learn his place and the respect due to himself, Mr Pargeter, as 'Chef' the title awarded to the head of a kitchen.

Antoine entered the kitchen on an inauspicious day: the sous chef had not turned up for work and Chef had a great deal of preparation to do by himself. He worked around the kitchen angrily but sinisterly quietly. The other staff stood about nervously awaiting orders. Antoine appeared in immaculate whites and carrying his own set of knives. It seemed to everyone that here was a professional. He nodded to the others and then, with a glance at Chef, proceeded to slice the mounds of beef standing waiting to be turned into beef stroganoff. Chef turned from stirring a sauce and regarded the new member of his brigade.

"OK," he drawled, "Now sort out the lamb chops." It felt like a challenge and, indeed, it was. Antoine began to prepare them in the French manner. "Like this?" he enquired?

"No," came the response.

"I'm surprised you don't do it this way. It is the way that Kaufman taught us all," Antoine responded mildly. "Oh well, chacun à son goût." He shrugged and resumed the task.

"Kaufman? You trained with Kaufman?" Chef was amazed to hear that his own personal hero had trained the newcomer. He had all Kaufman's books and had even once heard him talk at an event in the Edinburgh Festival.

"Oh yes. I did my time at Chez Maximillian in Paris."

Mr Pargeter blinked. "Well, we must have a chat once service is out of the way. In the meantime..."

He barked out a rapid series of orders to the staff and the kitchen was soon a blur of activity, a miasma of steam and delicious smells wreathing round the busy figures.

Later that afternoon, after a successful lunch time service, the two men sat in Chef's little office surrounded by piles of invoices and fluttering paperwork. The conversation started generally, then deepened more and more until Mr Pargeter found himself pouring out his lifetime's hopes, dreams and disappointments. He found the young man to be such a good listener and source of wisdom that he felt, for the first time in many years, or perhaps ever, that he had a true friend. Their shared interest in food formed a wonderful context for their discussion and he listened with widened eyes to Antoine's tales of Kaufman's kitchen. They talked long after the store closed and Chef set off home with a spring in his step, for once feeling refreshed rather than drained by his day at Murrays.

Over the next few weeks, Antoine initiated some interesting changes to Chef's well-known recipes. The little additions of this and that, the slight alteration to cooking times or seasoning led to very noticeable but welcome differences in the dishes concerned. Although they were, technically, the same, they tasted very slightly different and much more delicious. Chef basked in the glow of a new restaurant review that praised his adherence to old, familiar dishes but with a wonderful new twist. Antoine stayed quietly in the background and his diffident manner endeared him to all, from Chef himself to the humblest kitchen porter.

'Uncle Toni' arrived in the Toy Department with all the sudden noise and overall effect of a hand grenade exploding down there. It was a rather dark and dingy department with somewhat lethargic staff. It had been a very popular department in Miss Paterson's day but, now she had left, the staff seemed to have slumped into almost complete indifference to the excited children who were still brought in by parents and grandparents who remembered a visit to Murrays' Toy Department as a treat in their past.

Antoine, who had metamorphosed into the exotic Uncle Toni, caused a sensation among the children. Dressed in brightly coloured trousers and harlequin shirt and sporting a large red spongy nose and frizzy ginger hair, he startled most mothers and grandmothers by creeping up behind them and tooting a large horn. The children cried with laughter. The staff looked on helplessly at first, then it was all hands on deck to man the tills. Antoine's cheery engagement with the customers led to a huge increase in sales. He would individually befriend a small child and, with the parents' permission, lead them round to the toys most likely to be suited to the child and to the pocket of the accompanying adult. This suited everyone and children clamoured to return to the Toy Department just to see Uncle Toni. He began to perform clownish tricks and to entertain groups of children while the parents shopped in other departments.

His time in the Toy Department was an unqualified success. He only left after ceremonially handing over his lurid suit and accoutrements to Andy, the youngest member of the Toy Department staff, earnestly urging him to keep up with the silly behaviour as children these days needed all the laughter they could get.

Antoine fitted in perfectly to any and every department he was assigned to. At the management team meeting Miss Murray marvelled at his success.

"Not only has he got on well with a very disparate set of staff groups, but he's actually increased turnover in each department."

"Wish he'd gone to more departments then," Mr McElvey replied sourly. He was suspicious of the friendly young Frenchman, as he tended to be of anyone with a degree of social facility.

Ignoring this and warming to her theme, Miss Murray continued, "He demonstrated tact and diplomacy to Mr da Costa, kept the porters happy…"

"No mean feat," said Mr Soames.

"…and helped to improve the catering, as well as making big changes in the way the Toy Department worked." Miss Murray was very impressed. "And all along made friends of everyone on the staff."

"He's such a handsome young man too," sighed Mrs Pegram.

"Shame he's gay then," snapped Barry Hughes jealously.

"Gay? No he's not. He certainly cut a swathe among the girls when he was with the porters, you should hear what Jim had to say about it!" Mr Philipson felt compelled to add. Barry glared at him.

"Margaret, he lives at Rosehill, you'll know him best of all. Once and for all is he a ladies' man or not?" Mrs Pegram asked.

"Well I don't know," she began. "We don't see much of him really. He's so self-effacing he doesn't want to be any trouble to us. Just disappears at weekends. He's very charming and extremely polite, of course, so I don't like to ask where he goes. I assume that he has some friends locally, or a girlfriend… or boyfriend." The latter was directed towards Barry who smiled smugly.

"Be that as it may," began Mr Philipson. "The

boy's an asset to the shop. Do you think he might stay on if we asked him?"

"Good idea." Mrs Pegram was keen to recruit him to permanent staff. Miss Murray happily concurred.

She thought for a while, "Do you know, I think I'll give his mother a ring. I met her a few times when I was working there with Antoine's dad. It was many years ago, though..." She hesitated, remembering a rather frosty dinner party. Madame had been uncomfortable with the young woman spending so much time with her husband. Certainly, Miss Murray had carried a torch for 'her' Antoine, the father of the young man in question. He was long dead of course, but some vague resentment towards her might have lingered.

She made up her mind. "Yes I will. Antoine's done so very well here. She should be proud of him and might appreciate hearing of his success. I could sound her out about the possibility of him staying on. They will probably have plans for him in their store but it's worth asking. I'll phone her tonight." The meeting moved on to other matters.

That evening, Miss Murray had resolved to speak to Antoine himself about the possibility of prolonging his stay at Murrays. However, when she asked Mrs Glen where he might be, it transpired that he was either gone out or had not yet returned from the store. His movements remained a mystery to Mrs Glen who liked to know exactly what was going on in her domain. She was beginning to be a little irritated at his elusiveness.

"Not to worry. He's a young man, I expect he has other fish to fry on a Friday evening," Miss Murray reassured her. "I'll be phoning his mother later. I just wanted to speak to him first. Doesn't matter though." Mrs Glen frowned. International phone calls were very extravagant and rarely made from Rosehill. "None of my business of course," she told herself with a sniff as she whisked out of the room.

Miss Murray turned with a sigh of satisfaction to her well-earned glass of chilled Chablis. "Friday evening at last," she thought. "I deserve this."

The unfamiliar ring tones reminded Miss Murray that she was phoning Paris as she listened for a reply. She glanced at her watch, forgetting for a moment the time difference between Scotland and France. Finally, her call was answered by a male voice speaking rapid French. At first she thought the number in the address book must be out of date, but she soon realised this was the butler.

She started out in hesitant rusty French, "Est que c'est possible…"

The butler rapidly recognised a non-native speaker and briskly cut in. "Madame is not taking calls just now. Who shall I say telephoned her?"

"Oh it's just, it's Miss Murray phoning from Scotland. I don't know if she'll remember me. I'm phoning about Antoine. I want to tell her how well he's doing here." There was a pause. She became aware of a whispered conversation going on at the other end of the phone. Then a woman's voice cut in.

"Good evening Miss Murray. I remember you well. How kind of you to call." It was Madame. Her icily polite tones echoed down the line.

"Oh well, it's a pleasure," Miss Murray gushed. "It's been such a long time since we met I wasn't sure if you would remember me."

"But of course. It was on his way to spend time at your store that…"

"He's done so well here. We're all so pleased with him. What a charming young man. You must be so proud of him." There followed a long pause. Miss Murray could hear an old clock ticking in the background. Trivially, she remembered an old clock with roses painted on the dial in the hall there. She wondered if it was the same one. The ticking continued. She stared at the receiver, frowning. Had the connection been lost she wondered.

Eventually, there was a response. "What do you mean that he's done so well with you?"

"Just that really, he's got on so well with everyone and certainly been an invaluable asset in several departments. We don't want to let him go," she finished on a cheerful note.

"But he has gone. Gone. He's gone forever. My Antoine is dead."

"Oh I'm so sorry, I didn't mean your husband," Miss Murray continued, confused.

"Neither do I. Antoine. My son, Antoine, was killed on his way to the airport to get the plane to Scotland. Damned Scotland. I wish he'd never heard of it." She spat out. "He would still be here with me if he hadn't tried to go there." She finished in a flurry of French, its general meaning unmistakable.

A hundred thoughts ran through Miss Murray's mind. It didn't make sense. None of it made sense. If he had died, then who was the young man who had caused such a stir in the shop? She became aware that the phone call had been terminated at the other end. She sat down with a thump on the nearest chair. Who was that young man? Who was this chameleon? A chimera?

Sometimes there are no answers. Her eyes filled with tears. Whoever he was, he had supplied just what was needed in every department in which he had worked. It was horrifying to contemplate that he was dead. Her thoughts reeled. Eventually, it occurred to her that Antoine was still, apparently, around. She picked up the phone again.

The next day Antoine presented himself in Miss Murray's office. He found himself seated in front of Miss Murray and Mrs Pegram both grim-faced

"Now Antoine, or should I call you something else?" Miss Murray opened.

He had the grace to look abashed in the face of such implacable hostility. "I see. I see you know about me." His assurance slipping visibly. "I can explain."

"Do so."

He took a deep breath. "I knew Antoine. He was my boyhood friend, but he grew apart from me as we grew up. You see I was the chauffeur's son, not the great son of the great household. I watched him though. From my humble position, I watched him. I saw how he spoke, how he dressed, how he treated people. I worked in the family department store in Paris as well. I saw how things *could* be done, how they *should* be done, but no one would listen to me. Why should they? I was a nobody. I never had the opportunity to influence change. It was so, how do you say... frustrating.

"I knew from my father, who still worked for the family as Madame's chauffeur, that Antoine was coming to work for a while here in Murrays. Such a wonderful opportunity, the sort of opportunity that would never come my way. Then..." He faltered finally.

"Then you decided to take advantage of his tragic accident?"

"Oui. Yes." He hung his head. "I know it was wrong. I'm so sorry. I stole the letter that was addressed to Miss Murray telling her that Antoine, the real Antoine, wouldn't be coming and why. I tried not to be a burden at all or to take advantage of your hospitality at Rosehill. I knew I could work hard to repay your faith in me at Murrays. I should have known it wouldn't work out. How could it?" He raised his head suddenly, his eyes blazing in what was either self-reproach or hopefulness.

There was a long pause while the ladies thought about the situation. With her head, Miss Murray thought that they should snap up this exceptionally useful, potential staff member, but her heart said a resounding no. They owed that to the bereaved family. They certainly couldn't take on this impersonator of their lost son, however good he was at his job. She shook her head.

Mrs Pegram said quietly, picking up the conversation, "No. You're right. We can't take you on." His head dropped.

"But you're so talented in this field." She appeared deep in thought then, "I can see how difficult it must have been to stand by and watch Antoine, the real Antoine, have all the opportunities while you never had any."

He nodded hopefully again. Suddenly, things seemed to be going his way.

"Now Antoine… what is your real name by the way?"

"Marcel."

"OK Marcel, how would you feel about working in another, similar store?"

"You mean in Glasgow or maybe London?"

Miss Murray interrupted, "I was thinking of New York actually Mrs Pegram. I can certainly arrange that for him."

His eyes widened. "Really? You would do that for me?"

"I don't see why not. However, don't for a single moment think that we're condoning your behaviour in impersonating the real Antoine. It was a terrible thing to do."

Suitably chastened, he agreed.

After a short while discussing practicalities and arrangements, he left, bowing deeply to the ladies. "Thank you from the bottom of my heart for helping me. I will always remember and appreciate this."

As the door closed behind him, Mrs Pegram turned to her friend, "Do you know, I think that is the first and only time we've ever seen the real Antoine/Marcel? He's always been someone else. Someone that was needed in each department. What a chameleon he is."

Miss Murray agreed.

Chapter 16

Rosehill Revels 2

You are invited to attend the annual staff tea party at
Rosehill on Saturday 15th September.
2.00pm–5.00pm. Please arrive promptly.
Tea will be served at 3.00pm.
Appropriate footwear may be appreciated.
No RSVP required.

The annual invitation to Murrays' staff tea party in its new format led to much discussion in the canteen. A copy was slipped into each pay packet at the end of August.

"What's the point of arriving promptly at 2pm if we're not getting any tea till 3pm?" One aggrieved voice asked.

"I know. The whole thing's usually so boring anyway that the tea is the only reason for going at all," said another.

"And what's all this about appropriate footwear *may* be appreciated?" chipped in a newcomer to the conversation.

"Cheeky besom. Is that her way of saying that our high heels might damage that precious lawn of hers?"

"Her housekeeper is a right nippy sweetie. Bet she's put her up to it." They all agreed and comfortably settled back to deploring the macaroni and glaring at junior staff in too short skirts.

There was no question of them not attending. The invitation to the annual tea party was in the nature of a royal command. No RSVP was required as, basically, there was no choice. Staff were expected to attend.

Surprisingly, the attitude of the management team, with certain obvious exceptions, largely reflected that of the floor staff. They were not looking forward to the event at all. Even Mr Philipson, who could usually be counted on to be relatively upbeat, seemed downcast at the prospect. However, he hid his misgivings. "We'll just have to pin on the big smiles and support Margaret," he said with a wry grin. They all tended to refer to Miss Murray as Margaret when she wasn't there. It was unlikely that she would have objected to such informality face to face but somehow no one could bring themselves to risk it except, perhaps, Mr McElvey, who had known her since she was a child. She occasionally forgot herself and called him Ian. They all speculated from time to time on the relationship between the two and noted that he was invited to dinner at Rosehill on a fairly frequent basis. Kindly Mr Soames had always explained it away as Miss Murray feeling sorry for Mr McElvey living in what he called 'a home,' as if his prestigious club residence could be called that. The others remained unconvinced.

The great day dawned bright and sunny. This was forecast to remain all day, a great relief for Miss

Murray and the house staff. Looking out of the kitchen window at breakfast, Mrs Glen remarked, "Well, no need to set up in the garages this year anyway, we can use the big lawn." To her surprise, Miss Murray, who had joined the Glens for breakfast claiming she needed an early start, responded, "No, actually I'd prefer it if you kept things the way they were last year. Set up the tea table in the garages. Oh, is that the time? I'll need to get going."

With that she got up and left the room by the back door. A van could now be seen on the driveway and Miss Murray hurried towards it.

The kitchen party looked at each other, then Mrs Glen shrugged, "Wonder what she's up to? She was just saying last month how boring she'd found last year's do."

"A magician?" Mr Glen offered hopefully. He loved a conjuror.

"No," scoffed his wife, "They're just for kiddies' parties." She saw he'd sat back to relight his pipe. "There's no time for that. Go out to see what she's up to. We've got our hands full enough getting the teas all organised."

Grumpily, he followed orders. She tied on her apron and grimly braced herself for the day's events.

Outside, Miss Murray was directing the van men to set up their cargo at the side of the big lawn. A small platform was built and a tent erected to one side of it.

As they laboured back and forth with the tables and chairs, Mr Glen and Mr Joshi, now joined by the management team and a few volunteers from the shop staff, looked at the new set up on the lawn.

Mr McElvey tried to give the lofty impression that he was in on whatever the surprise was, but the others were doubtful.

"So what exactly is going on then?" queried Mr Soames directly.

"It's not for me to say." Mr McElvey fobbed him off expertly.

"Well I'm off to find out," said Barry, putting down his load of folding chairs and sauntering off towards the lawn. He returned almost immediately. "No luck. All they could say was that they were to make the delivery and set it up."

The management resumed their tasks and soon all the tea tables and chairs were set up on the driveway near the garages. Mrs Joshi, Siri and Mrs Glen could be seen ferrying the tea things and putting them out on the trestle tables in the triple garage. The bunting had been put up the previous evening and everything looked festive.

After a brief respite for lunch, the managers and the staff helpers left to change into their more formal tea party outfits. Meanwhile, having already changed, Miss Murray and Mrs Pegram conferred on how best to organise the afternoon. Two secret VIPs had already arrived and were comfortably accommodated in the tent with the flap firmly secured. They had run the gauntlet of Mrs Glen's scrutiny but she could ascertain nothing useful from the two nondescript men each carrying holdalls and one with an oblong box.

It was decided that Mrs Pegram would greet the staff as they arrived and direct them straight to the lawn. Miss Murray would be waiting for them, standing on the platform. She wanted to give a little speech of thanks for the sterling efforts of the staff before introducing the main event of the afternoon.

"Oh Margaret. Do you think it will really be all right?" Mrs Pegram was worried. "Some of them are not as young as they were."

"It'll be fine," her friend reassured her. "They'll enjoy it." The two women, after a last check in the long mirror in Miss Murray's room, descended the staircase and went out into the garden ready for the event.

Mrs Pegram stationed herself by the large gates and firmly directed the initial trickle and then the increasingly large torrent of staff over to the lawn. The staff of the various departments milled about aimlessly, wondering what was going to happen. Ladies in higher heeled shoes discreetly changed them as directed in the invitation and some of the men removed their overcoats.

It was getting pretty warm. The garden looked its best, the flower beds bursting with colourful blooms and some ladies looked longingly towards them and the benches placed at intervals around the garden.

"I'm too old for all this standing about," complained Miss Piper from China and Glass. Others nodded in agreement. Some of the younger staff were actually sitting on the grass and chatting unconcernedly. They were used to doing what they were told. The staff from Menswear were getting more and more desperate for a cigarette. "For God's sake get on with it whatever it is," groaned one through gritted teeth. Hearing this, Mr Philipson turned from his place near the front and fixed him with an icy glare. Nothing was said, but it was easy enough to extract his meaning. Time wore on.

Eventually, Mrs Pegram nodded to Miss Murray to indicate that the bulk of the staff had arrived. Miss Murray stepped to the edge of the platform and a hush descended on the waiting crowd. There was a perceptible move forward. The youngsters scrambled to their feet, brushing off loose grass.

Miss Murray began. "Ladies and gentlemen, firstly how nice it is to see you all here again. If this is your first time at Rosehill, welcome. I hope you enjoy your day."

She smiled towards a group of the younger men women and to Anjuli and Samantha standing together at the fringe of the management group. They smiled back in pleasurable anticipation.

"Now you're probably wondering what all this is about." She indicated the tent and the lawn. There were nods. "Well I'm going to try to explain, but I think it would be better done by Mr McPhail."

At that, the tent flap opened and a small man in

an outdated army uniform festooned with medals stepped onto the platform. Muttering broke out all around.

Miss Murray continued: "Mr McPhail is going to tell us about a famous dance: the Reel of the 51st. His grandson, Mr Upton from China and Glass, was telling me about it and I was fascinated. I think you will be too. After that we'll all have a well-deserved tea."

The muttering reached a crescendo. Mostly negative. How boring. A historical talk. The porters glowered mutinously from the very edge of the crowd, planning an escape. However, the little man moved to the front of the platform and began to talk in a quiet West Highland accent.

He began to tell them of the brave exploits of the Gordon Highlanders and how the 51st Highland Division were captured after fierce fighting, and were eventually imprisoned at Laufen, a POW camp in Bavaria. To help alleviate the boredom, one of the officers had started to run Highland dancing classes on the roof of the prison hospital. Some officers from other captured divisions joined in and a reel club was formed. The men enjoyed this form of exercise and the bored officers began to think of different dances to teach them. Eventually, they came up with the idea for an entirely new one. It was to be a dance based on the Saltire, the badge of the 51st.

By this time everyone was silent, leaning in towards the little man telling his tale. People looked toward each other and nodded appreciatively. A fine story. What had it to do with them though?

Everything became clear when Mr McPhail finished by saying, "And so ladies and gentlemen, today we're going to re-enact what happened then.

"We're going to dance the Reel of the 51st."

There was an immediate outcry. Calls of "I can't do that," rang out. Miss Murray moved forward and smoothly announced that they would indeed at least try and that Mr McPhail would guide them through it at walking pace. There were grudging nods and sighs as Mr McPhail, now speaking in a loud commanding voice, called out, "Ladies and gentlemen take your partners please." Everyone looked around for a partner. Several ladies immediately joined hands as there were far more ladies than men among the staff. In the general hubbub, Mr da Costa could be seen trying to slope off. Susan called after him.

"Not now, Susan," he replied irritably.

To everyone's amazement, she bellowed, "Yes now Martin. Come here at once. We're going to dance this." Surprising his mother and her partner, Mrs Garland, he turned meekly round and joined her.

Over in the management group, Barry immediately triumphed by capturing Mrs Pegram's hand. Seeing that she had no choice, she smiled and the two of them stepped forward. Mr McElvey offered his arm stiffly to Miss Murray who took it with dignity and joined the others. Sets were being made up all over the lawn. Mr McPhail was much in evidence as he moved among them directing them into place. From the relative security of the tea urn in the garage, Mrs Glen and Mrs Joshi looked at each other. Before a word could be spoken, their respective spouses stepped forward, "Shall we dance?" said Mr Glen to the consternation of Mrs Glen.

"Why not dance with Mrs Joshi?" she suggested indicating her friend. "Give her a change from Indian dancing?"

"What a good idea," said Mr Joshi, moving towards Mrs Glen, "In that case you must give me the pleasure of this dance." Swept up by his courtly offer, she awkwardly agreed and the two couples crossed over to the lawn to find a set to join.

Spotting the escaping porters, Mr Soames called out, "Now then gentlemen, which of you would like to partner the ladies from Cosmetics and Perfumery?"

These ladies, in their customary heavy make-up, looked decidedly uncomfortable. Each had been hoping to catch the eye of Flash Harry Ferguson, late of Menswear and now a key member of the Ladies Separates team. However, they good naturedly accepted the proffered hands of Jim and his staff and formed sets. The staff from Menswear had found a quiet spot for a smoke, but stubbed out their cigarettes and hastened across the lawn to snap up the more glamorous female staff looking for partners. Flash Harry, to his dismay, had been captured by Mrs Hope from Model Gowns.

"I've been waiting for this moment," she told him with a wink. He quailed.

Once the sets were made up, Mr McPhail walked them through the steps. The key section being when a large St Andrew's cross was formed by the couples in each set. They stepped and counted and stepped and counted, all at walking pace. Mr da Costa found that he enjoyed the structure of this sort of activity and felt secure with Susan as his partner hissing instructions as required. He saw her in a new light. He liked it.

After a while, people began to be a little bored. Rueful eyes were cast towards to the tea area. However, when Mr McPhail was finally satisfied, the tent flap opened and out stepped Ewan the porter, unrecognisable in full Highland dress and carrying his bagpipes. At a nod from Mr McPhail, he struck the pipes and commenced the traditional tune for the Reel of the 51st: 'the Drunken Piper'. As the lilting pipe music echoed through the air, its magic revitalised the weary staff. The counting and stepping and counting and stepping gradually transformed into dancing. Suddenly they were dancing. They were all dancing. Heads were thrown back and faces were wreathed in smiles. Mr McPhail shouted encouragement from the platform, "That's it ladies and gentlemen, that's it, that's it!"

Joyous cries of, "Gaun yersel," and the traditional, "Heeugh," rang out as they all birled and skipped through the dance's formations. Cardigans and ties were abandoned and shoes slipped off altogether for the pleasure of dancing on grass in bare feet. Catching her breath briefly, Miss Murray berated herself for not thinking of a photographer. This was such a wonderful moment it was a pity not to capture it. However, she didn't think she'd ever forget it, the time that the entire staff of Murrays, department store of distinction, two hundred of them, danced on her lawn. Her breath caught momentarily in her throat as she thought about it. It was wonderful.

In twos and threes, the older ladies hirpled off complaining, albeit smilingly, of throbbing bunions and nipping varicose veins. "Well that's me had my exercise for the year!" laughed one. "It was great though. Took me right back to the church hall dances when I was courting," said another.

One by one, the sets slowed to a standstill and Mrs Glen and Mrs Joshi rushed over to the tea table ready for the onslaught. Siri Joshi, who had watched the whole thing from a window above the garage with Bluebell at her side, now shuttled from the kitchen to the tea table with big jugs of orange juice for the thirsty dancers.

On the lawn, the final sets were slowing and the valiant piper finally finished his last reel and put down his pipes. He smiled towards Mr McPhail who inclined his head in recognition of the lad's piping skills. The two went back into the tent where an excellent bottle of whisky awaited them in the traditional way.

The noise level at the tea tables was colossal. Everyone was talking and laughing at the tops of their voices. Any ice was long broken and people chatted to the managers as though they were old friends (which, in many cases, they were). Moving from table to table gulping down the cold orange juice, Miss Murray was thrilled to hear how well her surprise had gone down with the staff.

Mrs Struthers told her, "It was the most enjoyable thing I've done in years. It makes me think that we should do more of it." She looked around at the other ladies sitting at her own and nearby tables, "What do you think girls? Should we set up a reel club of our own?" On the receipt of enthusiastic nods all round she turned back to Miss Murray, "Looks like you should get the prize for initiative this year," she jokily informed her. Miss Murray smiled.

By 5pm the last stragglers were walking wearily out of the big gates to catch their buses home. Everyone agreed that the afternoon had been a great success.

Back at the house after the final chairs and tables had been stored away, the tea cups, saucers and plates washed up and the final crumbs thrown to the birds, the management team and the house staff relaxed. Sitting in the kitchen, Miss Murray looked worriedly at Mrs Glen. "You've overdone it," she scolded fondly, "I told you to have a seat and leave the hard work to the youngsters."

"It'll be a black day when that happens," was the sharp response. Miss Murray shook her head.

Grasping an awkward nettle, Mr McElvey pointed out, "You're a fine one to talk Margaret. When will we be sitting back and letting the youngsters take over?" He was in a mellow mood, partly due to the tiring exertions of the afternoon and partly due to his helping Mr McPhail and Ewan finish the bottle of whisky. Barry had found him sitting by himself in the tent as the men came to fold it away.

"Less of that talk Ian. I'm surprised at you," Margaret reproved him. Sensing the slight change in the happy atmosphere, Mrs Pegram poured her friend another glass of Chablis and suggested they repeat last year's fish supper. This suggestion was enthusiastically taken up and Barry set off with a list.

Later that evening, sitting by herself at the fire in the study, Miss Murray contemplated the day. It had gone so well. It had been wonderful to see the entire staff group dancing the intricate figures together. They worked so well, staff and management, together producing and running an efficient and valuable business. Another year had passed at Murrays. The management, with the hard work of the staff team, had steered the old store through some difficult times. A strike had been circumvented, dangerous exposure on public media had been dealt with and the customers had remained loyal. Neither births, deaths nor difficult relationships had held back the progress of Murrays. New staff had been recruited and promising youngsters had been earmarked for greater things. Innovative ideas had been developed and all the indications were that new horizons beckoned and Murrays would, indeed, remain a department store of distinction and could still assure customers of its best attention.

She stood up, stretched, turned off the table lamp next to her and, calling for the cat, continued up the stairs, sure of a good night's sleep. Back to work on Monday...

The End

Acknowledgements

Profoundest thanks, as ever, are due to the wonderful people at Comely Bank Publishing without whom this book would never have seen the light of day. Especial thanks are due to Emma Baird, who was the editor for this book and who made such excellent suggestions in such a tactful way. Thank you, Emma!

Grateful thanks are also due to Gordon Lawrie at Comely Bank Publishing for arranging all the various technical aspects related to publishing as well as his tireless promotion of my books.

Where would I be without readers? I am most grateful to Maureen Hope the most encouraging of fans: my first ever reader. Fortunately, there have been many more. Throughout the past year I've been fortunate enough to meet very many people at author events who have enthusiastically embraced Murrays and all who sail in her. I've heard wonderful reminiscences of the old days in shops like Murrays. Such stories!

As ever I must thank my family. My husband Paul has been ever encouraging and supportive. My children and their families have been interested and happy to comment on suggested storylines. Last of all, Baz, my giant cat, has quietly supervised every word I have written.

About The Author

Jane Tulloch was born in Edinburgh and has lived there ever since. For 30 years she worked for the NHS as a psychologist in the field of adults with autism. Before that, however, she worked in a large department store which provided the inspiration for the Murrays series of books. Her first book, *Our Best Attention*, was published in 2016.

She lives with her husband, giant cat and occasional welcome interruptions by boisterous grandsons.

Further resources for *Assured Attention* and other books, as well as information about the author, including contact details for Jane herself, can be found at www.janetulloch.com.

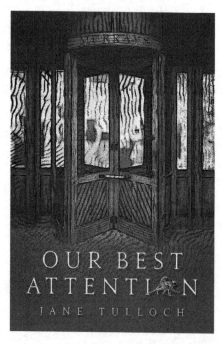

Our Best Attention by Jane Tulloch begins the story of Murrays department store, a fictional Edinburgh department store in the 1970s. It's a large, gothic, rambling building, but the store's real heart lies in its staff and its customers. Join the owner, Miss Murray herself, as she tries to manage the challenges Murrays faces in adapting to changing times.

Four Old Geezers And A Valkyrie

Gordon Lawrie

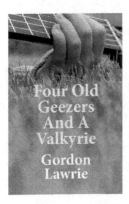

Four Old Geezers and a Valkyrie by Gordon Lawrie is an entertaining romp set in contemporary Edinburgh. Brian, aka 'Captain', is a recently-retired, disillusioned teacher who has split acrimoniously with his wife. A chance meeting with his best man encourages Captain to dig out his 40-year-old guitar which leads to a series of hilarious jam sessions. Posting the results on YouTube, the songs prove to be surprise hits...

The Man From Outremer

T. D. Burke

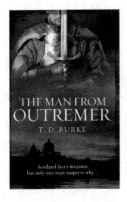

The Man From Outremer by T.D. Burke is a swashbuckling tale of treachery and action. Set largely in Scotland at the time of the early Scottish Wars of Independence around 1300 AD, it follows Derwent, a Scottish Crusader turned-clergyman, and his involvement in the Fall of Acre in Palestine, then as Prior of Rosslyn in Scotland.

Katie And The Deelans

Emma Baird

Katie and the Deelans, Emma Baird's first Young Adult novel, is the story of Katie Harper and her friends, ordinary teenagers who go to the worst school in the country. Life, however, takes a turn for the extraordinary when Katie and her friends take up magic lessons. Taught by the fabulous Miss D'Azzler and the enigmatic Jazz, Katie and her friends have a lot to learn about life, friendship and love.

Weekender

Roland Tye

Set in Edinburgh's recent past, Roland Tye's debut novel **Weekender** follows the intertwined lives of a series of the city's residents. As the life of each very different character touches the next, we move through the weekend discovering a city of contrasts: a city of wealth and poverty, drugs and desire, sex and not a little love, despair and redemption.

About Comely Bank Publishing

Comely Bank Publishing (CBP) is a co-operative publishing house giving bright, new talent a platform.

Founded in 2012, CBP aims to tackle the quality issues faced by traditional publishing, i.e. the concentration on books only by established authors or bankable names. CPB helps new authors publish at low cost and makes no profits from its authors.

Comedy, historical fiction, young adult fiction and more – Comely Bank Publishing covers many genres and we are sure you will find a book you enjoy…

All books are available in print and e-book formats on Amazon, Kobo and other outlets, as well as in Edinburgh bookshops and directly from the Comely Bank Publishing website:

http//www.comelybankpublishing.com

And finally...

Did you like this book? Why not review it?

Reviews are important for books, especially books published by small, independent publishers such as Comely Bank Publishing. Why? They help our books get found.

How do you choose a book to read? You might choose it because it's prominently displayed, you've seen an advertisement for it, you know the author's work or you've read a good review.

Small, independent publishers do not have the same budget for marketing as traditional publishing houses do. We can't afford posters in railway stations or pages in magazines and we don't get access to the same number of book stores.

However, sites such as Amazon, Kobo and GoodReads can level the playing field for independently-published novels. Book reviews act as "word of mouth" for shoppers online. They provide social proof that something is good – well, at least if your reviews are positive!

The more reviews a book has, the further up the rankings it moves. A book with a lot of reviews will come up quickly if a reader types in 'Scottish novels' or whatever genre to the search engine.

You don't need to write a long or detailed review – just a couple of sentences will do.

Thank you!